LIMITS FROM THE WITHIN

Verses Kindler Publication

Verses Kindler Publication.

Website: www.verseskindlerpublication.com

LIMITS FROM THE WITHIN

By: Ms. Rudhrapriya Sritharan

ISBN: 978-93-5605-047-1

FICTION STORIES 1st Edition

Price: 249 INR

INDEX

DISCLAIMER

"LIMITS FROM THE WITHIN" is an anthology that comprises different write-ups written by twenty-four wonderful people from different parts of the world regarding their take on "mental health". This anthology consists of all kinds of genres, some of which include short stories, poems, experience sharing and articles. All the names, characters, businesses, places, events and incidents in this book are the product of the author's own subjective and research work, done to the best of their knowledge and abilities. Any resemblance of an actual person, living or departed is purely coincidental. The content present in the anthology is the original literary piece of the writers and as a compiler; I have tried my best to make it plagiarism-free. In case if there's any plagiarized content, the author is solely responsible for it; the compiler or the publisher would not be held responsible for it. All the literary pieces written in the anthology is written with immense love and dedication towards spreading the word regarding mental health. In case anybody's sentiments get hurt it is purely unintentional.

ACKNOWLEDGEMENT

Firstly, I would like to give thanks to our publisher "Verses Kindler Publication" for providing us with this wonderful opportunity and platform of being able to publish our literary pieces and share them with the world. I extend my sincere gratitude to Kashish Chadha, Preethikha and Diksha for constantly guiding me throughout this entire journey, this would not have been possible without their genuine support and patience. This book is dedicated to everyone dealing with something of their own! You will come out stronger and unstoppable like never before, be sure to get help when needed, YOU MATTER!

I would wholeheartedly also like to thank all the incredible writers for being a part of this wonderful journey. Every writer has written their piece with hard work and love, their unparalleled support and dedication has made this book a beautiful and inspiring one. I owe a very greater part of the credit to all of you who have believed that I could do this and helped in making it a smooth and enjoyable journey filled with memories and lessons. I would also like to take this opportunity to provide my sincere gratitude to my family and loved ones in general for believing in me, without their wonderful support and guidance, I wouldn't have got here. Lastly, I would like to thank all my readers for giving us this opportunity where we could express our feelings and thoughts and present them in our literary pieces.

PREFACE

"Mental health," is a phrase or term that individuals often misunderstand or overlook. There are very many factors behind one's mental well-being. This anthology consists of different variations of it, such as the mental health factor of bullying, mental abuse, disability, colourism, body-shamming and etcetera with a whole lot more considering the fact that mental health is something that is very vast. Behind this anthology is a wonderful team of writers expressing their take on it through words. Writing is one amazing way to express how one feels and to spread a message that will eventually help someone.

YOU ARE NOT ALONE!

"Mental health is not a destination, but a process. It's about how you drive, not where you're going." -Noam Shpancer, PhD

"Just because no one else can heal or do your inner work for you, doesn't mean you can, should, or need to do it alone."- Lisa Olivera

"What mental health needs is more sunlight, more candor, and more unashamed conversation." -Glenn Close

If you want to change the world, pick up your pen and write" - Martin Luther King

TRIGGER WARNING!

Events regarding

mental abuse, bullying, death & suicide

are included in this anthology!

COMPILERS PROFILE

-RUDY S @ RUDHRAPRIYA SRITHARAN-

Selangor, Malaysia.

Meet The Compiler!

Meet here Rudhrapriya Sritharan, the compiler of this book. She goes by Rudy for short, she resides in Malaysia and had just completed her Diploma in Information Technology. Rudy has co-authored prior to this. She developed her love for writing and as for her it was more so of therapy to heal, she states. She enjoys writing on her writer's page on Instagram @peace.soul.quotes. She believes that writing is another way of self-expression. Here she brings to you this anthology regarding mental health to spread more awareness.

One's mental health journey is something close to heart for sure and no one is alone in this. It's all about being together, creating this unity of a safe place with genuine intentions for others to get inspired and move forward happily with a positive mindset. ***YOU MATTER!"***

Warmest regards,
~Rudy S

Instagram: @peace.soul.quotes
LinkedIn: Rudhrapriya (Rudy S) Sritharan
Email: peace.soul.quotes@gmail.com

More About Mental Health In Regards To The Book

The book is titled **"LIMITS FROM THE WITHIN"**, and from that, the moto that I bring along is to enlighten people more about the mental health factors and sides of things that others may not know of, see and understand. Also, with this, many can get more knowledge from what's **within**, in this case, within refers to **"mental health."**

In addition to that, the book is written by people from all around the world and has many thoughts and ideas included in it. With it being "mental health" as the theme and with an open genre, one will be able to discover a whole lot from this book. This book consists of parts that include death, feelings, spirituality, and etcetera. It's also great for **self-motivation!**

"ME!"

The Lows!

Mental health was always something that was close to my heart from a young age because it was something that I struggled with, only at that time I didn't really know what it was and the best thing to do about it. When I was younger, I didn't know what things meant and was told to move forward, but something within me was always unhappy, never satisfied and always held back.

I went through depression and anxiety! There was a time when things were very devastating, it was hard to move on and leave everything behind that was bothering me. Times were really tough! I still remember the time I couldn't get out of bed, now you're probably thinking that "hmmm, this girl must be really lazy!" Laziness wasn't the issue here! A negative state of mind was where I was at! I didn't intentionally do that, **I was depressed!** I had my little support system at home along with fur buddies to put a smile on my face, but deep down I was still so **numb!**

Even society tends to think the worst beyond disgrace of that. **Depression** in other words is a lack of motivation, things that once excited a person no longer will enthusiast the person, it's the feeling of numbness that revolves around the past. This feeling is like there's no way out and it can last for days, weeks, months and even years!

Anxiety was another thing that killed the living soul out of me! Now if you have anxiety, you'll know how it feels! I can't really put my finger on it, but I'm sure it's the past events that triggered all of that. Sometimes, what happens is that past trauma can affect how you see your future, and that's where you start panicking and constantly think about what's going to happen and have worries that eventually cause anxiety!

What made me unhappy was being bullied. Bullying can open up many different gateways of yourself that you didn't know existed as it will make you see yourself in ways you never saw yourself before! This can cause a lot of trauma, anxiety and depression. Mental abuse was also something that I saw and went through since young. People who have been through it know how it is. For example, being gaslit and when you finally come out and speak about it, people say that you're imagining and assuming, being around narcissistic personalities that tear you apart from what you really are just to stand out amongst the crowd. There is a lot more within the mental abuse aspect, such as guilt-tripping, victim blaming and sexual assault. People who have been there see the world differently, it's a long-term type of trauma that does make one become a better judge of character though after going through it all.

Moving on, with having anxiety and depression, it always would make me lose my appetite, I fell into a bad lifestyle pattern that caused me to skip my meals and eventually I became ill. When you skip your meals, you'll invite lots of complications regarding the human anatomy, I'm not going to get into anything deeply biology related but stomach problems revolving acid reflux was what got to me. This ended up affecting my respiratory system, all due to acid reflux which is really dangerous! Do you see how from one thing, it just goes to another? Like in this case, well-being affected physical health which attacked the human anatomy and then it led to respiratory issues.

The Overcoming Stage!

Throughout everything, I had myself backing me up, I never gave up. This made me become more **self-motivated**. Even though there was all of that tragedy, I had myself throughout all of it! And this is what I stand by right now.

FOCUSING ON MYSELF!
BELIEVING IN MYSELF!
TREATING MYSELF NICELY!

All of that may sound corny, but without practicing all of that, you will find it really hard to come up and reach miles later on, trust me!

This whole writing journey of mine came along one day when something clicked in my mind and I told myself that "I don't want to be like this anymore! I want to change all of this! I'm going to start writing!" I would write quotes regarding things that are close to my heart and post them on my Writer's page on Instagram. I turned all of my feelings and emotions into fuel to help me. **THIS REALLY WORKED!** It brought me into a whole new headspace.

Until today, when I look back at it, it seems like all of those bad things that happened really happened to me for the better of me! It's true what they say!

"Sometimes good things fall apart so better things can come together"- Marilyn Monroe

At that time, I felt so miserable, I was suicidal, I wanted to give up, I was at the lowest low of myself possible, but I'm glad I didn't give up! At that point, I always asked myself and the people around me, "Why me?" Well, the answer to that is ***"It's not how we fall. It's how we get back up again- Patrick Ness"!*** Next time you ever question why something bad ever happened to you, ask yourself this,

"What if everything that happened here, happened for a reason?"- John Locke

How It All Came Together!

I have my downfalls and so do you, but **NEVER STOP TRYING! NEVER GIVE UP! AND ALWAYS BELIEVE IN YOURSELF!** I promise you, no matter how hard it is, **things will get better!** Another thing is to always surround yourself with positivity. **Cut out all of the negativity! Toxic people, toxic cycles and toxic surroundings,** just let it go, it is going to take time and mental strength but **try! Just take** in the **good** and **leave out** the **bad**! That is something else that you can do **for yourself!**

Lastly, **self-motivation** is **very important! SELF-MOTIVATION** is the thing that will make you go forward. No matter the age, whether you're single or in a relationship, have kids or not, **self-motivation** is the thing that will allow you to go far in life! Self-motivation also includes the **confidence** you carry with you, **that is the grace** that will hold up your **crown!**

Well then, I hope everyone here has learnt a thing or two and gets inspired! Enjoy some awesome write-ups from these twenty-four wonderful people! They're amazing!

Oh, and don't forget to check out their links as well!!!

KEEP GETTING INSPIRED AND KEEP LEARNING!!!

“POETRY RELATED TO MENTAL HEALTH”

Hidden Pains

Once you break the heart,
then nothing can reduce its pain.
Then over time, we act as if we have forgotten,
but we know that the pain is still hidden deep in the heart.

Now we fake our laughs to make people think
we're not in pain,
but the pain is evident from the tone of our voice.
And now we try to socialize with others
to cover the pain,
but the pain is evident from the look of our eyes.

The Last Collapse

The worst wait is to wait at the end of the road,
and the hardest decision is the one
that you will make at that time.
Because you know you have reached the end,
and the signs of your collapse have begun.
No one left beside you,
you lost some,
and life distanced some.

Pain In Other Words

Getting used to the pain is different from feeling better.
Living in pain for too long can make you forget
what it means to be well.
Pain changes you.
It makes you look at the world from another side.
And after a while,
you won't be yourself.
You will become a better version
of what you were before.

Be Gentle

Moving on is hard,
but it's not impossible.
It will take some time,
but it will be over.
Just seek to do it in the right way,
do it without breaking anyone's heart.
Try to leave a good remembrance about you,
let them remember you as an affectionate person.
A person who was gentle when he left,
just as how his presence was.

The Other Side

For once, I'll try to do everything wrong.
For once, I'll try not to be a good friend.
For once, I'll leave everything without trying to fix it.

I did everything right, and yet I ended up falling apart.
I did everything right, but I ended up with a broken heart.
For once, I'll do the opposite of what I did.
I'm wondering about the result of the other side.

-ABBOUD DAWOOD-

Ankara, Turkey.

Abboud Dawood is an engineering student, co-author, poet, and writer. He was born in Iraq and lives in Turkey. He is interested in many areas such as writing quotes, poems, short stories, etc. He loves to write on the theme of life, nature, beauty, happiness, motivation, and inspiration. The journey of writing started after suffering from a long illness and having three unsuccessful surgeries. He found comfort in writing words that cannot be spoken aloud.

Email: abboud.dawood@gmail.com
Instagram: @abboud_dawood

"MISCONCEPTIONS AND INNER CONFLICTS"

Mental health seems like such a big word that is associated with the well-being of us both mentally and emotionally and anything about mental health has only been taken seriously only since a couple of years ago. Even after so many years of acknowledging it, still some people think of it as rather insaneness and something made up than to understand the real meaning of it. There are way too many factors that affect us or at least there are way too many things that we as individuals worry a lot about and it is this that paves way for one being emotionally detached, anxious about taking decisions, being critical of oneself, being insecure, feeling inferior and many such factors leading to depression and other serious ailments which might be left quite unnoticed. There have been campaigns that occur in order to promote the importance of one's mental well-being yet, there are so many people who are unable to figure out or even accept the fact that they are undergoing something traumatic because of the expectancy to keep moving on without figuring out what went wrong and end up having no claim over themselves.

Why is mental health being given such importance or at the very least why is everyone talking about it? Is it really worth the hype given to it? I had once encountered a similar question being asked and compared to the times when such terms were not really used. The fact or the truth is that they might not have used a fancy term to describe their stress, emotional outbreak, or any such factors but would have definitely come across a certain situation which might have crumbled them and the result of it- them having to hide it or trying to act completely normal as if it was a daily occurrence and failing to confront it (the emotion or the situation). Just the concept of mental health sometimes sounds so abnormal and defective for some people even in the 21st

century we live. The thought of someone being mentally broke and emotionally detached is viewed and judged as something that one has to take responsibility for all by themselves rather than lending them a helping hand.

There are so many reasons as for which one may cause a wreckage to his/her mental health and suffer through it but what makes it worse is having to listen to the judgements of society and sometimes of those people, so-called our relatives or friends or anyone who do mean anything and everything to us, judging us for every little possible thing that could have happened sometime without the least idea of what is going on within us or without the least slight notion of how broke we are.

I truly don't know or understand how many people who lived before us had coped with things that we still find it hard to express. Whether life was any different for them, did they not put any serious thought into it? or is it us who complicate things which is what I hear a lot from the people who had lived and certainly end being called irresponsible (young people in general) for the choices I make or choose? Of course, everything might have been different in the past than it is in the present. The competition in every sector of life is just too fierce as we have various needs and necessities and sometimes fall back without having the means of acquiring it and those without the means or the money might someday find it through various ways and will always end up better but the ones that are broke from within always end up with a space or a vacuum created within them that can never be filled or at the least filled anytime easily.

The society that we live in today or in a time period that we have grown has always shown and projected things that are important or at the least should be kept in priority according to the judgement of the masses or the elders, which primarily includes the people to whom we are born, the ones we are born with, and many others who we come across in life and tend to give importance just because we were told so. We are sometimes more obliged to prove to the world than we prove to ourselves. Of course, there are many situations in life where we find ourselves giving in the custody of our lives to others just to let them know how much they mean to us or the other way around. But honestly, are there ways in which one can predict the behavior of a person just because they seem to think that they have known all about the person right from the beginning and shared a more private space than others, definitely not that I think there can almost never be a moment where we can tell that we know absolutely every inch of a person as we are mostly stuck up in the midst of finding ourselves and have never really reached our destination yet. If it is anyone one has to be so sure about, then it is surely ourselves that we should have known all along, not others.

It is the way we have been fed up with things from a very small age as to put people before us which is not really a bad idea but those are the people, even if they are one's parents who have lived a different life in a different time period and have become a totally different generation with a thought process not so similar to that of their own children, and not really trying to understand or give importance to the thoughts of one's children not in all cases but in some cases though. Many adults of today neither get into relationships nor get married because of the traumas of their past or more probably because of the way they were treated and were made to feel in the relationships that they were asked to blindly believe and end up having problems of commitment. A lot more people have so many things hidden within themselves very well, that even their closest or dearest acquaintances have no idea about what they have gone through. The fact that one suffers trauma or undergoes a rough path in life emotionally, doesn't really mean that they deserved it or gained it through their actions but it's because of the way we were tuned by so many things or at least the things that we witnessed, as of to keep our priorities which being mostly to forget our own will and wish.

But anyhow we have come to a time where, even though it's hard to choose for oneself, we still choose different paths, different ways of life, ideologies to stick up to and do what feels the best for us. The ones who might have studied with us or were of our same age group might have gone in different directions-some married, some working, some studying. And probably in the eyes of society, they all have figured out what they want or what they need in life, more accurately, what society thinks one should possess. But there are also a certain group of people who might have been left behind from it or might as well have chosen to be left alone, who might have lost their way, stranded at some point of time, which definitely doesn't happen with their choice.

Not everything in the world can be figured out at the very first impression of it. We all need time and space for ourselves to get to where we want to go. By far, living in an extremely patriarchal society and in a very conservative family I have always been reminded or said that a woman requires no to less private space as she is required to put others before her always and that the freedom given to me was way too much and a blessing, while most of the eyes have forgotten or more simply set aside the fact that we might always want more of what we truly deserve- to be ourselves. It might seem rude for not feeling gratitude towards what I have been bestowed, but there can always be the want within us for more and better things. We are sometimes made to feel sorry for the things we actually don't feel sorry for, treated like a mere speck of dust and call it a blessing, called abnormal simply because we choose different things than the rest and distinguished as problematic only for the way we differ from their opinions or more exactly when we defend our views.

It is not that they (the world, society or the elders) are not able to see what we are, but they most probably try to ignore the fact that we can be better as an individual and so are definitely better, than what they think. It might not be the same in everyone's place but definitely, most of us could agree with this, as most households in our society work this way. For most of our lives, we try to impress people and mostly it is them who don't try to see the real us and demean us for what we really are.

Everyone wants to grow to become a better person than we were yesterday, but why are there so many parts within us that we have to leave behind or sometimes sacrifice and become mentally and emotionally broken? Why are we questioned for every little thing- when we have an emotional outbreak? We are called aggressive, violent, someone who cannot control themselves, or if we end up crying, called a crybaby and are asked to be strong. We definitely have names to be called when we end up having either of one reaction or anything different as well. If being strong does really mean hiding our emotions and acting normal, then I don't really think I can be this person hiding myself to escape from being judged. The hardest way in order to get to anywhere in the world has to be growth and betterment without sacrificing any part of your conscience or compromising yourself to the ideals of the world, but that's what we are made to do most of the time. It certainly doesn't need to be done only that way, as it wasn't why probably we were created, only to leave our parts behind or go on suffering.

What is done can surely be undone, even if it was our mind that gave out, there might come a time where we could let all those things that hurt and broke us within be left behind us and when the vacuum might be filled with memories. Different things work for different people- but mostly it is time that brings an end or lets us begin things and more importantly it is better to confront ourselves with the truth about ourselves than to hide in a lie which can be safer for a little while but not for the life one intends to live.

We might not always know the cost of one's happiness- what one may have gone through to become what they are, so it is always better to not judge and if only possible treat them with a little compassion than pointing out the difference one possesses and come together to share our stories how much ever it was considered a worthless one by others. We all are a part of this world how much ever we have lagged behind or left us behind, we all can still be happy with what we have become and where we stand.

- Almass Banu. S

-ALMASS BANU-

Tamil Nadu, India.

Almass Banu is currently pursuing her Law degree in "Dr. Ambedkar's Global Institute of Law", after having completed her Master's in Literature. Started from knowing nothing about literature to completing her undergrad program in Bachelor of Arts and her newfound love for Literature made her to move forward. She then completed her Master's of Arts in Literature, at "Women's Christian College, Chennai". She desires to acquire her Doctorate someday. She is very much curious in learning about people and also wishes to take up Psychology. She is a great lover of art, music, literature and loves to read books of various genres as she thinks it reflects people's life. Also, she likes to write down her thoughts on various things from time to time.

Email: almassbanu3498@gmail.com

"SELF-LOVE AND YOU"

A life-changing force has the full-bodied celestial power to ignite your life and grant you all the inner peace and happiness you've ever desired. This powerhouse cosmic gift, is the almighty self-love.

What is self-love? One may ask. Self-love is as simple as it sounds with tremendously deep, dark and personal complexities, unique to each of us. Self-love is gentle, scary, profound, gritty, emotional, mundane, fun, challenging, and transformational. Yet, most of all, self-love is beautifully life-changing. Self-love isn't beautiful in the same way as anything else. For the hearth of its majesty lay in each and every one of us who decides to embark on a self-love journey. Therefore, its beauty can never be defined by one word because its very essence is a fascinating multiverse of unique experiences.

Part of the beauty of self-love also lies in the fact that self-love is for anyone and everyone. One doesn't need anything aside from an open mind and heart in order to embark on an epic self-love journey.

Perhaps one may ponder, why self-love? Well, why the hell NOT? Self-love provides the individual with an abundance of inner strength, inner peace and love. Eventually, the practitioner of self-love experiences its power and quite often wants to share it with others and with the world.

If anyone outside of yourself has poisoned your mind into believing that any part of you is unworthy or unlovable, leave those thoughts in the past where they belong and reclaim your inner power! You're always worthy of self-love regardless of your sex, gender, race, ethnicity, skin colour, sexual orientation, diet, if you think a hot dog would be considered a sandwich or not, your feelings about Crocs, mental health struggles, your weight, where you're from, how much money you have, how badly you've messed up, your past, or literally any other reason not listed! The reasons can go on forever but hopefully, the sentiment is clear, everyone under the sun, here on Planet Earth is worthy of self-love! A planet where more people love themselves instead of suffering in the crippling waters of self-hate and negativity is a dream, and hopefully someday, a reality.

Negative emotions are bound to creep up, as this is an inevitable part of the human experience. However, self-love enables one to navigate through tough mental spaces all the better. When one becomes their biggest cheerleader, miracles happen. Are your pom-poms ready? Okay, you don't need to wear a short skirt if you don't feel like it, but please do become your biggest cheerleader! But you must, first and foremost, LOVE YOURSELF!

Here are five ways to begin loving yourself:

1. Recognize the need to practice self-love.

Identify why you'd like to start practicing self-love. The reasons could be anything from desiring to be more confident, leaving a toxic relationship, or struggling with other issues. Every one of us has a dark side, and that's okay. Many times, it is through our darkness that we realize just how brightly we can shine. Maybe you're tired of your cynical attitude, self-sabotaging behaviour, or being too loving to others and leaving little love for yourself. Congratulations if you realize that you'd like to change for the better and love yourself through the process!

2. Commit to practicing self-love

Self-love is a practice. Think of self-love as a lush garden that needs constant sunshine, weeding, and watering to thrive. The more you practice tending to your self-love garden, the better you'll become. As you evolve into better versions of yourself, the needs of your self-love garden will change. You must make a serious commitment to loving yourself every single day. EVERY DAMN DAY! Some days will be hard. If you feel like you don't love yourself on those days, all the cells in your body care very much (they're working hard just for you), as do your loved ones. Self-love is a lifestyle and a daily practice that needs a serious commitment with all strings attached!

3. Incorporate self-love into your daily life

Once you've committed to loving yourself, you must incorporate it into your everyday life. The ways in which you can depend on your unique individual needs. We can all practice self-love by getting the proper amount of sleep each night (7-8 hours), eating a well-rounded and nutritious diet, and staying adequately hydrated. Make a vow to end any self-bullying. Your thoughts and mind have power. Use that power for good. Say good thoughts to yourself after a bad one. Or, don't give too much power to bad thoughts as you typically would. Ask yourself, how can I show myself some love today? Seek the answers. Showing yourself love could mean going for a ten-minute walk every day or finding the strength to leave a bad relationship. Whatever the specification, make it happen!

4. Be authentically you

To love yourself, be authentically you! Celebrate your originality and don't worry about anyone else. The person who matters most is you! Comparing ourselves to other people is as easy as spending too much time on YouTube or Instagram. However, don't forget that there is NO ONE ELSE exactly like you on the entire planet. Rejoice in that fact! Let your freak flag fly! There are no official guidelines telling you that you have to be like anyone else. Don't hide your true self out of fear that you won't be accepted. You don't want acceptance for an inauthentic presentation of yourself only to face rejection towards the real version. The right people will accept you no matter what. GO BE authentically YOU!

5. Accept yourself

Accept the parts of you that you enjoy flaunting to the world AND the parts you don't. I'm talking about accepting the good, the bad, and the ugly here space cowgirls and cowboys. We've all made mistakes, and have character flaws. Truly forgive yourself for past mistakes. What's gained from constant guilt trips? It may take some time to forgive yourself, and that's okay. Listen to the song Please Forgive Me by Bryan Adams. Perhaps that will help. If you're not a Bryan Adams fan, maybe serenade yourself by singing, "I love you. I'm sorry. Please forgive me. Thank you." If you don't feel like doing either one of those suggestions, I'd say, okay, don't forgive yourself and be miserable. Just kidding. Take that crap out to the garbage alongside that duck sauce from last month! As for your flaws, the good news is that if you put in work, you can improve upon them. It's up to you! There's always room for self-improvement, and that's a beautiful thing. It's easy to accept the parts of yourself that you and other people admire. Working your way through the murky waters of your mistakes and character flaws is a courageous act of self-love. Reflect on areas of improvement as a rewarding path to morph into a better version of yourself. If you have mental or physical ailments, be gentle with yourself. Please don't beat yourself up. You deserve SO MUCH MORE than that! Treat yourself the way you would treat someone you love. Your mistakes, character flaws, mental and physical ailments don't make you any less of a gorgeous celestial being with traces of the heavens inside. Accept yourself for all that you are! Your mind, body, and soul are counting on you to begin and to stay loving yourself. The universe supports you in your self-love travels. I support you too! We can do it!

Self-love is also a significant aspect of mental health. YOUR MENTAL HEALTH MATTERS! Always has, always will. It matters even if you may not know how to properly weed out the bad thoughts and water the good. You'll figure it out and wake up one day to a garden with weeds that don't overgrow. You reap what you sow. So, try your best to look for the good. Your mental health matters today and way beyond into the wild far-reaching corners of space.

Feeling too much can be a handful but it can also be your greatest gift. Make that shift, from viewing your faults as your downfall to seeing them as a path to rise up. Transform the darkness into light. Send those labels into the nearest black hole, and SAY IT WITH ME, "MY MENTAL HEALTH MATTERS."I MATTER. ALWAYS. PERIOD."

I sincerely hope you start on your self-love journey if you haven't already! Never underestimate the power of smaller steps in your self-love journey. Any small steps you take in the exploration and understanding of what self-love looks like to you, will add up over time, and accumulate with brilliant self-love victories, discoveries, and healing. Furthermore, don't forget that everyone's self-love journey is different, so what works for me may not work for you and vice versa. Don't compare your journey to someone else's! I hope your self-love journey is as healing and magical as you allow. Happy self-loving to all you wondrous, Cosmic beings of love! We were made to love, so go LOVE YOURSELF!

-AMANDA ROSE DIXON-

New York, United States of America.

This here is Amanda Dixon and she's from Long Island, New York. She's very passionate about sending the message of self-love to as many people as possible and hopefully helping some along the way. She loves writing, animals, her family and friends, music, nature & fitness. She genuinely believes if people love themselves more, the world will be less dark and brighter, just like the stars in the sky.

Please feel free to visit my Blog,
Planetselflove.com

Amanda Rose Dixon

Instagram: @planet_self_love
Facebook: @Planetselflove
Pinterest: @PlanetSelfLove88

"FINDING BUBBLES OF JOY IN DAILY LIFE"

Bubbles of Joy

Introduction

I remember as a child the fun of blowing bubbles. They were shining globes of rainbow colours floating up toward the sun. My friends and I would run and try to catch them or simply watch them sail higher until they disappeared.

What was so captivating about these bubbles? They mesmerized for a glorious moment and then were gone. Poof! The wonderment of it.

Many childhood memories are like that… captivating, absorbing, and fleeting.

As an adult, I appreciate these interludes that provide a respite from life's busyness and responsibilities. It's pure enchantment to peer out my window and spot a hummingbird visiting the salvia plants or the wild turkeys that randomly appear, prancing across my yard.

My heart and spirit are touched at the sight of a full moon over the ocean, a gorgeous sunset, and a beautiful smile from a loved one or stranger. I call these impermanent snapshots of time "bubbles of joy."

Below, I offer a few sweet moments to savour and ideas on how to incorporate more joy into your daily life.

The Energy of Hummingbirds

Have you ever been enchanted by a hummingbird visiting your garden? It is hard not to stop whatever you are doing and watch this amazing little creature feeding off the nectar of any brightly coloured flowers you may have nearby. A tiny hummingbird beats its wings fifty to eighty times per second, can hover and fly backward, and feeds from hundreds of flowers a day!

May the hummingbird inspire greater vibrancy so that you, too, will enjoy good energy as you set about the tasks you have planned for your day.

Ideas for you:

1. Take frequent breaks if you sit at a desk. Stretch and take a walk outside.
2. Drink more water and focus on eating foods that are brightly coloured like the flower's hummingbirds love (think blueberries, apples, strawberries, salad greens, carrots, beets, etc.).
3. If a creature as small as the hummingbird can accomplish all that it does, imagine what you can do! Get out your journal and write down some dreams you have for your life. No dream is too small or too big.
4. Experiment with your wardrobe. Adding bright colours to your outfits and accessories may help you feel more confident and add a little zip to your every step.
5. Play some great music and dance around in your living room. Like a hummingbird, rotate your arms quickly (a great upper-arm toner), move forward, backward, and to the side… Have fun!

Good News Has Arrived!

How do you feel when you receive good news about your life or about something good that has happened in your community or the world? Your son or daughter got into the college of their choice. You got a raise. You just found out you are expecting your first child. Your favourite sports team made it to the championship.

When we receive good news, we experience a burst of excitement. I know I would rather have more good news in my life than the alternative. A challenge for us all with social media and the 24/7 news cycle is that we can get stuck in the negativity that often comes with the media. Too much exposure can affect your mood and health. There is a way out!

I believe that the more you look for good news in the media and in your own life, the more joyful moments will show up.

Ideas for you:

1. When someone asks you how you are doing, always respond with something positive: "I am great," "All is well," "I can't complain," or "It's a beautiful day!" When you approach someone, ask them: "What's the good news?"
2. Give yourself the gift of a media diet from time to time. Block out times of your day or perhaps a day out of the week when you do not read or listen to the news. Take a break from social media too. Consider putting your phone away as you near bedtime, and instead, take a bath or read something soothing or inspirational… or just get lost in a great story.
3. When you do read your newspaper, magazines, or articles on your phone, look for the positive and inspirational stories. They do exist! Seek them out and you will notice a measurable improvement in your mood, energy, and outlook on life.
4. When good news shows up in your life, celebrate and appreciate it!

Orange Sherbet and Vanilla Ice Cream

What flavour of ice cream did you love as a child? There are certain foods and flavours that just bring us back to the simple pleasures of being little without a care in the world. What are those foods for you?

Ideas for you:

1. Visit an ice-cream store or buy a flavour of ice cream at the grocery store you have not eaten in a long time. Order an old-fashioned banana split, milkshake, or sundae next time you dine out.
2. Prepare a favourite childhood dish and share it with your family.
3. Visit a gift shop that has those nostalgic candies and snacks from another era. These seem to be more popular these days, and it is so fun to see that type of candy bar you used to love but don't normally see much anymore.
4. Just enjoy (and don't worry about the calories)!

<u>Uncontrollable Laughing Fit</u>

Have you ever gone into an uncontrollable laughing fit and you suddenly find yourself on the floor with tears flowing out of your eyes? Often when this happens, it comes on quickly and unexpectedly. It usually does not last long… but what a delight. To lose yourself in laughter is a wonderful bubble of joy! There are many health benefits to laughter. Laughter has been known to improve mood, decrease pain, and release stress and tension. It is fun to let go and not always have to be so put together. The people around you are bound to relax, too, and perhaps get in on the fun. Permission to be silly is a precious gift you can give yourself.
Ideas for you:

1. Spend time with people who make you laugh.
2. Read or watch something funny.
3. Practice letting go of the need to judge or worry about what others think of you.
4. Do something that is just plain wacky or fun: jump on a mini-trampoline, whirl a hula hoop, dance to some silly music, make faces at your kids, spouse, or pets.
5. Even if you don't feel silly, try laughing anyway. Laughter yoga enthusiasts do this, and it can change the whole chemistry of your body.

The Sweetness of that Last Jigsaw Piece

I just love jigsaw puzzles! They relax and stimulate my brain in an easy, soothing way. I believe our brains love patterns, and there is something fulfilling about turning 1,000 pieces of chaos into an orderly and beautiful picture. To succeed at this task, you must decipher patterns and then organize the colours, designs, and shapes of the puzzle pieces. At first, it can be overwhelming, but gradually you see the bigger picture coming together. Once on a roll, it is very satisfying as you put those final pieces together. Then the last one… ah! The piece de resistance. Formidable!

An added note: Completeness is highly rewarding, and when you finish a puzzle, it is so fun to admire your achievement.

Ideas for you:

1. Ask yourself what areas in your life feel chaotic to you and perhaps are stressing you out? How could you focus on them and give them the order that you deep down yearn for?
2. Get out your journal and ask yourself these questions: Is the journey or destination more important? In puzzle terms, do you enjoy most the final reward of completing and seeing that beautiful accomplished complete puzzle, or is just getting there the most satisfying part for you? I encourage you to not think too hard or self-edit. There is no right or wrong answer here. Just write and explore for yourself.
3. When it comes time to choose puzzles to work on, what do you prefer? Abstract designs? Landscapes? Perhaps something whimsical? This is just something interesting to note, and it might be fun to experiment with different types of puzzles.

4. Even if you are not a jigsaw puzzle fan, I invite you to remember a time when you solved the last word in a crossword or word search puzzle or figured something out that had been perplexing you for some time. How did you feel?

Oh, Sister and Mama… Your Beauty is Still There

(Originally posted on July 20, 2022, on my new blog Menopause: The Journey)

Oh, Sister and Mama,

As you sit and rest this evening….

Know that you did some good, you did your best, and if you were challenged in some way today – well that's okay.

Know that the woman staring back at you when you look in the mirror tonight as you brush your teeth…

Just KNOW that she is as beautiful as always and radiates God's love and energy as she always has. She loves you and she yearns for you to love her.

Oh, Sister and Mama,

Do not worry about the wrinkles you see or the fatigue in your eyes. That just means you put in some amazing years and a meaningful and well-spent day today. Tonight, you will rest well and tomorrow you will look at that beloved face that you have spent your whole life with, and you will see just how beautiful she is.

Your beauty is still there. Inside and out. Now more than ever.

DEBRA DIPIETRO

Florida, United States of America.

A Message from Debra:

I feel honoured to be a part of this special project, she states. Mental health has always been a topic near and dear to her. She was always a sensitive child and even throughout her adult life, she has off and on been challenged with people pleasing, social anxiety, and now dealing with the effects of menopause.

This is an interesting time for the world. Many people are still trying to regain a sense of normalcy after the Covid-19 pandemic. 2+ years of social isolation, wearing masks, losing loved ones, worrying about our own and our family's health, businesses closing, plans getting cancelled, etc. has impacted our mental health in countless ways.

Here in the United States, we are grappling with unprecedented political divisiveness, gun violence, and globally the effects of economic uncertainty and climate change, she adds.

It makes one want to crawl into bed and never come out!

That is where the pages above come in. She simply offers you a few ways (*Bubbles of Joy*) to focus on and incorporate more joy into your daily life. Hopefully, at least for a while, she can help lessen the anxiety that many are feeling.

At this writing, she's almost 56 years old. For 6 years she had been dealing with hot flashes and all the physical and emotional challenges that come with this change in life.

Menopause has been very challenging for her and her mental health. She knows she's not alone. Therefore, she ended by sharing a verse, *Oh, Sister and Mama... Your Beauty is Still There*, dedicated to all her sisters out there who are members of this "club".

Menopause may not be talked about too much but half of the humans around the globe experience it at some point (there's no avoiding it) and it's some comfort to know that we are not alone.

Thanks for sharing the journey with me!
With regards, Debra DiPietro.

Author of *Short Morning Prayers A Collection of Heartfelt Prayers to Start Your Day*
Jacksonville, Florida USA
LinkedIn: Debra DiPietro
Email: DebraDiPietro@Outlook.com
Instagram: @debradipietro
Twitter: @WarmMilkJournal or @AtMyEase
Pinterest: Debra DiPietro
Facebook: The Warm Milk Journal
Website: DebraDiPietro.com, TheWarmMilkJournal.com & MenopauseTheJourney,com

Not The Real Me

how can I hide myself forever
behind those baggy clothes?
behind the sophisticated makeup?

is it not me that you crave for?
or is it just the idea of me?
is it the long and silky hair of mine?
that it is drawing your attention
little do you know the bottles of serums
emptied to achieve it

why do I have to
take so much effort
into becoming someone I'm not
I don't have perfectly silky hair
for the most part
It's tangled and rough just like your thoughts

or is it the way I dress?
wish I could just step out
wearing the first thing I get my hands on
why do I change 100 outfits before finalizing?

don't you love me for who I am
or for what you think is perfect
in a world full of pretenders?

Long Gone

all this while
wishing to disappear
into thin air
but deep down
all that I longed for
was a gentle breeze to
caress me and
whisper
you will make it through.

You Are

you are not your tears
you are the **courage**
that lifts you up
every time a tear rolls down.

you are not your falls
you are how high
you **rise** after it

you are not your fears
you are how you
face it

you stand **strong**.

Author's note

The above poems are merely words that I needed to hear when I was at my lowest, but instead what I got was just bare silence. It shows how important it is for people to listen to positive affirmations when they are at their lowest. It is going to play a major factor of preventing them from taking rash decisions and causing harm to themselves. It is vital that we extend a helping hand and make them realise how important they are to society and to their loved ones.

-DHIVYADHARSHNI-

Bangalore, India.

Dhivya is a uniquely creative and passionate person. She has a great interest in visual arts and basketball, and has recently discovered her interest in poetry and literature. Her work is freestyle with a mix of wordplay, emotions and whatnot. She states that she is inspired by the wonderful people in her life along with all her experiences and memories. To get in touch with her, do reach out to the following below.

Email: dhivya.07renga@gmail.com

Instagram: @dhivyarenga_

"THE INTEGRATION OF SPIRITUALITY AND RELIGION INTO PSYCHOTHERAPY"

Introduction

The integration of spirituality and religion into psychotherapy has been a source of debate in the field of psychotherapy or counselling for decades. Several people have written on the subject but to date, other practitioners in the mental health field tenaciously adhere to the belief that spiritual issues should not be discussed with clients if they arise in counselling. So, the debate about the phenomena still lingers on. This chapter looks closely at matters of spirituality and religion and their inclusion in psychotherapy. It also discusses the bifurcation of psychotherapy, the renewed interest in spiritual interventions in counselling, and the rationale for including spiritual or religious issues in psychotherapy.

Spirituality and Religion Defined

Spirituality may be defined as the capacity and tendency that moves the individual toward knowledge, love, meaning, peace, hope, transcendence, connectedness, compassion, wellness, and wholeness.[1] The concept encompasses a variety of phenomena, including experiences, beliefs, and practices, and it is also approached from a variety of perspectives, including psycho-spiritual, religious, and transpersonal.[2] By comparison, religion is defined as "an organized belief system that includes shared and institutionalized, moral values, beliefs about God, and

---

[1] Muller, Geri. *Incorporating Spirituality in Counselling and Psychotherapy. Theory and Practice* (River Street, Hoboken: John Wiley and Sons, 2002), 6.
[2] Ibid, 6

involvement in a religious community."[3] According to Blalock and Holden, a person may possess a spiritual experience either within or outside the context of a religious system. They also stress that even though spirituality and religion are related, the two concepts differ, in that spirituality is a more inclusive term.[4] The different views regarding spirituality and religion have emerged because of various worldviews through which people perceive the world and how they interpret what happens in their lives and the world. However, spirituality involves seeking connection with the ultimate reality. Some call this ultimate reality a Higher intelligence, a God, or Nirvana.

The Bifurcation of Psychotherapy and Spirituality/Religion

The bifurcation between psychotherapy and spirituality or religion has existed for ages. Plante observed that for a long time, psychology has often excluded any discussion of spiritual or religious issues in practice."[5] Surprisingly, prominent figures in psychology such as William James, Carl Jung, and Gordon Allport were greatly interested in the relationship between psychology and religion.[6] Collins asserts that for many years professional counsellors focused attention on dealing with all issues that clients raised except for religious issues because they were thought to be irrelevant or pathological. Additionally, textbooks in psychology, psychiatry, and counselling often tend

---

[3] Walsh, F.Beliefs, Spirituality, and Transcendence: Keys to Family Resilience. In M. McGoldrick (Ed). *Revisioning family.*Walsh 1998, 72

[4] Blalock, Sarah M, and Holden Janice miner. 2018. Preparing Students to Counsel Clients With Potentially Spiritually Transformative Experiences, *Counselling and Core Values* 63:18.http://onlinelibrary. wiley.com, 2018, 1

[5] Plante, Thomas G. Integrating Spirituality and Psychotherapy: Ethical Issues and Principles to Consider. *Journal of Clinical Psychology* 63, no.9: 891–902, 2007. www.interscience.wiley.com.

[6] Ibid, 891

to ignore the subject of religion, and its significance in people's lives and dismisses it as pathology.[7]

The counselling literature does not provide sufficient and concrete reasons for such an occurrence. However, others think that psychologists who opposed the integration of psychotherapy and spirituality into counselling were influenced by the sayings and perceptions of leaders in the field such as Sigmund Freud, B.F. Skinner and Albert Ellis did not take the study and practice of religion seriously.[8] According to Brock, professional counsellors perceived psychology as separate from and superior to theology as an academic discipline. The conflict between the two disciplines prompted psychologists to give preference to scientific research.[9] Furthermore, psychology viewed itself as a serious science and began to refrain from anything that looks like spiritual and religious to maximize the scientific approach to research.[10]The pursuit of scientific research was also enhanced by the fact that psychologists found matters regarding spirituality and religion difficult to study scientifically, as a way of providing empirical evidence to back up their assertions.[11] Consequently, spirituality and religion were not taken seriously by psychologists. Interestingly, psychologists who were interested in integrating spiritual issues into practice conducted that in secrecy for fear of being taken to task by opposers of the integration of spirituality into therapy.[12] This indicates that there has always

---

[7] Collins, Gary R. *The Biblical Basis of Christian Counselling for People Helpers*. Colorado Springs: NavPress, 2001),
232.

[8] Plante, 892

[9] Brock, Raymond T. 2006. *Introduction to Psychology: A Christian Perspective* (Springfield,
Missouri, USA: Global University, 2009), 389.

[10] Plante, 892

[12] Ibid, 892

been a section of mental health providers who believe in the importance of including such issues in psychotherapy.

The Renewed Interest in Spiritual Interventions in Counselling

In recent times, the wind of change has blown and it is perceived that the bifurcation between religion and science is softened and a renewed interest in spirituality and religion in psychotherapy has blossomed. According to Corey, literature in the counselling field indicates that many people want to explore their spiritual and religious issues in the course of therapy."[13] Similarly, Clinton and Ohlschlager also point out that previously any discussion of spirituality with clients has been challenged by counsellors but currently the situation has changed because professional ethics in psychology allow for the discussion of clients' beliefs and values in therapy."[14] Also, some major counselling organizations are beginning to realize the need of integrating spiritual issues into therapy. The organizations observe that spiritual and religious matters are therapeutically relevant, ethically appropriate, and potentially significant topics for the practice of counselling even in secular settings.[15] On the same, Lodge and Hofacker retort that counselling that fails to explore a person's spirituality misses foundational pieces concerning how an individual makes sense of personal identity, purpose, and sense of meaning.[16] Unfortunately, the field of

---

[13] Corey, Gerard, Theory and Practice of Counseling and Psychotherapy (Belmont, CA: Brooks/Cole, 2009), 452.

[14] Clinton, Timothy and Ohlschlager, George. 2002. *Competent Christian Counselling: Foundations and Practice of Compassionate Soul Care* (Colorado Springs, CO: Waterbrook Press, 2002) 332, .

[15]Corey, 117.

[16] Lodge, Chad and Hofacker, Heather. *Integration of Spirituality in Counselling.* Texas: Samaritan Counselling Center.http://Samaritan-counseling.com/. 2016, 2

counselling has procrastinated to respond to clients' spiritual and religious issues even though caring for souls needs to address the body, mind, and spirit. Many researchers also agree that spirituality is an important element of mental health and when it is included in counselling the treatment process becomes effective.[17] For this reason, spiritual issues need to be explored and integrated with other therapeutic tools in assessment and treatment to facilitate the healing process.

Reasons for the integration of Spirituality and Religion into Psychotherapy

To understand the need for the integration of spirituality and religion into psychotherapy, it is necessary to explain what the terms soul, spirit, heart, and mind mean, and how they relate to each other. According to Clinton and Ohlschlager, the term "soul" in Greek is *"psyche"*, which is translated from the Hebrew word *"nephesh"*. *Nephesh* refers to one's inner life, the self, or the living personality.[18] Furthermore, in the East emphasis was often put on the essential unity or wholeness of the whole person. For this reason, the term *nephesh* or soul is used interchangeably with the term "spirit" (*pneuma* or *ruah* in Hebrew), "heart" (*kardia* or *leb* in Hebrew), and "mind", which is *nous* in Greek.[19] It is concluded that the terms soul, heart, spirit, and mind refer to the same thing, the inner life of human beings that embodies the nature and essence of the spirit.[20] Consequently, whenever people fail to develop spiritually, the inner man suffers.[21]

---

[18] Clinton and Ohlschlager, 124
[19] Ibid, 124
[20] Ibid, 119
[21] Ibid, 120

Of greater importance is a relationship that exists between counselling and spirituality. Sawai et al. state that "therapy," a term that is sometimes used instead of counselling, originates from the word "*thereia*" which means "soul healing" and that by identifying the Greek word "*therapuien*" which means "to heal", then therapy is the art of healing[22]. Therefore, counselling means soul healing. According to Sawai et al., the goal of counselling is to heal the soul. The soul refers to the immaterial spiritual essence that is located in the core of the spiritual heart of the man's body.[23] As noted above, the terms "soul" and "spirit" are sometimes used interchangeably. It is not difficult to perceive how needful it is to approach people's problems from a holistic point of view. Given this, Clinton and Ohlschlager stress that during assessment helpers need to look at all dimensions of counselees including the spiritual dimension, thus making a diagnosis that also considers the holistic approach.[24] Blalock and Holden also postulate that attention to spirituality is vital to a holistic counselling process.[25]

Similarly, Benner and Hill perceive that spiritual or religious issues need to be included in counselling for the following reasons: first, both psychotherapy and religion focus on existential issues such as personal meaning, freedom, values, and suffering. Second, religious and spiritual issues are important to consider in psychotherapy because most people seeking counselling express a desire to discuss religious matters. They also observe that in the mental health marketplace, with lots of

---

[22] Sawai Perdani Rezki, Dini Farhana Baharudin and Muhammad Khairi bin Mahyuddini. 2015. *Integrating Spirituality into Counselling: An Insight.* https://www.researchgate.net/publication

[23] Ibid

[24] Clinton and Ohlschlager, 332

[25] Blalock, Sarah M, and Holden Janice miner. 2018. Preparing Students to Counsel Clients With Potentially Spiritually Transformative Experiences, *Counselling and Core Values*63: 31.http://onlinelibrary.wiley.com.

psychiatrists, psychologists, licensed professional counsellors, marriage and family therapists, and licensed clinical social workers, clients prefer assistance from the clergy because they believe that religious values are important for therapists to consider.[26]

Sawai et al. provide additional reasons for the integration of spirituality and religion in counselling.[27] First, the importance of spirituality in peoples' life has historically been ignored within the mental health fields because of the utilization of scientific approaches or positivism in the mental health field. Second, there is an association between religion, spirituality, and mental health. Studies have shown conflicting results regarding the relationship between religion, spirituality, and mental health. However, religion and spirituality have been shown to positively provide coping resources to people who are struggling with many problems such as physical or psychological illness, pain management, surgical issues, depression, addiction, and the use of alcohol and drugs, even though some studies reveal contrary results. Third, they stress that spirituality promotes wellness and health and also acts as a shield as well as a tool for intervention. In their discussion, they state that the spiritual disciplines of prayer, forgiveness, and meditation are used to facilitate the healing process in clients' lives.

According to Corey, people's spiritual values and behaviours enhance their physical and psychological well-being. It is clear that spirituality is an important component for mental health, and its inclusion in counselling practice can enhance the therapeutic process."[28] Plumb also observes that spirituality and religion improve rates of well-being and life satisfaction apart from decreasing rates of suicide, substance abuse, and antisocial

---

[26] Benner and Hill, 1150

[27] Sawai et al, 196

[28] Corey, 452

behaviour. However, he argues that for people who possess rigid religious beliefs based on sin and guilt, spirituality and religion deepen mental health problems such as depression, delusions, and hallucinations.[29]

Therapists need to provide enough support to assist such clients to deal with their issues. On the same, Lifespan development expert Santrock perceives that religion plays a role in adolescents' health and whether they engage in problem behaviours.[30] One study revealed that adolescents who were higher in religiosity were less likely to smoke, drink alcohol, use marijuana, not be truant from school, not engage in delinquent activities, and not be depressed than their low-religiosity counterparts. Finally, concerning the role of spirituality and religion in adults, researchers have also realized that religious commitment in adults helps to moderate blood pressure and hypertension. More importantly, some studies also confirmed a positive association between religious participation and longevity[31].

---

[29] Plumb, Alison M. 2011. Spirituality and Counselling. Are Counsellors Prepared to Integrate Religion and Spirituality into Therapeutic work with Clients? *Canadian Journal of Counselling and Psychotherapy* 45, no. 1:1-16. https://files.eric.ed.gov., 2.

[30] Santrock, John W. 2011. *Life-Span Development* (New York: McGraw-Hill, 2009), 388.

[31] Ibid, 492

-DR. JOSEPH C. PHIRI-

Lilongwe, Malawi.

Dr. Joseph C. Phiri is an ordained minister in the Malawi Assemblies of God church, counsellor, lecturer, and author based in Lilongwe, Malawi. He holds among others a Doctor of Religious Studies in Christian Counselling (Trinity College of the Bible and Theological Seminary-USA).

Facebook: Joseph Phiri (Chimowa)

Website: DJCP Counselling Consultant

"LAST HOUR OF THE NIGHT-MENTAL HEALTH & SUFFERING"

In the heave of my early morning drills, just as I approached the deserted portion of the sloppy Kisamis ant hills, my eyes penetrated through the sun's rays and settled on a seemingly dull-looking figure beneath the thorny bushes. Anxious to witness for myself what was happening, I fidgeted through the ugly bushes, and my eyes, acquiring a clear line of sight, made me notice the sideways movement of the purportedly human creature who seemed to be turning amidst agony and grief.

Who in my neighborhood could that be? I stopped to think of it. My often-unlucky reasoning smiled, eyeing another chance of betrayal. Today, however, I could be lucky, at least for once. I could spot someone by surveying my neighborhood in the most accurate of terms. I thought of my departed best friend and could attest those things haven't been easy for her people since she left. If I were honest with you, I would doubtlessly tell you how it hasn't been easy for me too. The troubled human creature resembled a woman, who I guessed, could be her mother. "Dear Leynah, your departure leaves mom with many rhetorical questions. More often than not, they crisscross my mind. I understand there would be no one to answer them regardless of how many times I ask or sit to figure it out. I guess not in this life; perhaps the afterlife," she shouted. A warry wail then rented the still air, accompanying the shouts; loud awakening echoes could be heard by those afar. For me, the weeping was too much to bear and before I knew it, I was yelling at her "hey STOP!" Starring helplessly, I observed her apple-red yet scary eyes that seemed to be warning me when she suddenly stopped, momentarily turning her covered head towards me.

Since her only daughter's demise, Caroline has never been the same woman the villagers knew before. She was suffering from severe mental health-related issues. More often than not, a random stranger could spot her visiting lonely places, seeking solace. The recent occurrences had made her believe suffering and torture bound the entire human habitation. Maybe for once, she was right. Just maybe. The God she served all her life might have forgotten or completely abandoned her. She promised herself to keep her distance from the land of the living. You could have heard the masses say her mental health was deteriorating.

Friends and family offered her all the emotional, mental, and psychological help she needed to restore her sanity. Additionally, they hired psychological doctors who conducted numerous counseling sessions on her. Despite all the efforts, nothing changed. Maybe she needed a little bit more of it or just something more convincing or just something else. Her emotional attachment to her seemed to have been too robust to let go. The birth of Leynah in the past two decades had given her a reason to live and perhaps be happy about what this life could offer. She raised her like a queen, chose to focus on her moral prowess, and reminded her of her value as a woman in society and how she could conquer the world.

Furthermore, Leynah, having been raised by a Godly woman, grew up a replica of her mother. Her strong personality and spirituality explained it all. Burying her head deep in thoughts, Caroline found herself a lonely woman. Leynah was gone and gone forever. 'Hodgkin Lymphoma,' the monster she is yet to come to terms with, had ruthlessly claimed her daughter's pretty soul at the beginning of the disastrous 2020 Coronavirus pandemic after efforts to fly her back to India for medication failed amid flight movement cessation.

After her first treatment back in 2015, Leynah may have proven to recover, though not fully, due to the side effects of chemo and radiation. Her immune system weakened. The illness made several friends distance themselves from her. As has been the tradition, fake friends flee. During such moments, one gets to know their real friends and family. The few, real ones, are a blessing in disguise. Such individuals unite for a common goal; to see you win the long battle. The brave girl fought till she was no more. Every day seemed a nightmare for a loving mother of Caroline's stature grieving her lost daughter. She wasn't used to the habit of not seeing or talking to her.

Caroline wasn't alone. Like a tremendous earthquake, the aftermath had triggered massive unrest among relatives and friends; new and old friends. I was no exception. The first six months had been a hell-on-earth for me. Just like any would-be victim, I couldn't tell who I was before. Being a research scholar, I had only learned in books and journals about what extreme cases of stress and depression can do to a victim amidst loss and suffering. But here I was, no more theory. I was practically that victim. Even though I wasn't myself anymore, I could recall how in one of the family gatherings, I overheard my uncle whisper to my mother how I had suddenly turned into a lunatic. I could later relinquish the few remaining pieces of my frail self in penning a poem, which I did in memory of Leynah. Believe me, it was a sigh of relief, having told the whole universe about her giant personality and how she lived on. Poetry is a magical cure, and I guess the universe deserves to know.

Recalling the events during her final sendoff, I had been privileged to mumble my last words; reminisce the old moments. The fallen heroine deserved all the respect. I gave her my last. In our local community, it was unheard of for a man to cry or become emotional during moments of agony and grief. I had even, at one instance, been showered with praises, having mentored some random kids who used to frequent climbing our mango trees to fall with a thud without showing the slightest of emotions. The situation here, however, could have been exceptional in a way. In my emotional speech, I confessed her remarkable possession of so great a personality. “Judging from the brief moments you’ve stayed with us, I am certain that no one regrets meeting you Leynah. Knowing you was the best thing that ever happened to me in this life." I paused to wipe the tears that had flooded my gloomy face. After a long battle with cancer in its early stages, you came back home, strong, like a soldier. I met you in one of the city's hotels for a chat. Shortly after exchanging greetings, death silence got the better of us. I read your mind and noticed you were in a dilemma. Looking straight into my frightened eyes, you asked to know if I could listen to your story. At first, I couldn't hold it, and I broke into tears. I reminded you that your life's story was worth hearing, meant a lot to me and that I was ready to hear it even a thousand times. It was all about your first successful fight against cancer. They will say you died, but I will surely prove them wrong since, as far as I know, you were only promoted to glory!" I concluded.

Lewis, the late girl's brother, also appended a short poem in loving memory of her, and her mother vowed to preserve such a piece of writing to reminisce her memories.

Brother, it's all magic; you always reminded me
My frail self-acquired the priceless motivation
To soldier on through this cruel life
While doctors broke the sad news to you
Like a lunatic, you laughed so loud

You laughed, always laughing amid trouble
And your brother noticed your weapon
To laugh and counter struggle
Your departure put mom in trouble
I will tell her to laugh

I gazed in utter surprise while you fought
Amazed at how strong you could fight
The monster that devoured your beautiful soul
The huge blows that seemed to make you fall
But like a wounded lion, you fought back

In your 17th surgery, they thought you passed
But I knew you from our past
Because later at midnight, you woke up and laughed
I know you still laugh to date
Even more with angels in heaven

Starring in admiration, I watched you struggle
I watched in tears, seeing you fade out of sight
I will refill my ink for the obvious reason
To write and paint you Leynah
Till your image gains breath

It was not until two years later when the depressed Caroline spotted a note embedded between the pages of Leynah's Bible while trying to go through her stuff. She knew that Leynah had intentionally left it for her. Curious to know what message it had carried, she quickly opened it but was cautious enough to avoid tearing it in the process. She shut the door behind her to ensure no one disrupts her when she buries her head into the written note. Positioning herself on the deserted bed, she began to go through it, reading it aloud, word by word. She cleared her throat and began, “It is quite a painful and heartbreaking experience as I shed secret tears seeing you sit beside my dead bed Mommy! Yes, this is my death bed! I have to admit to lying to you about my present health condition. Mom, you deserved some message of hope, even if it meant lying. I realized you would suffer long mental and emotional torture when I'm gone, and no one, even the seasoned psychological doctors, can ever dig out the eternal attachment we two have had. You've always been a strong woman, and I couldn't love you more. You willingly joined me in this battle, and sadly, however, this is the end. Be sure not to confuse this for a defeat since you understand I have fought this menace, though as a victim and won some battles. Please mourn not when I am gone; stand with people living with cancer worldwide, campaign for early cancer screening, and all measures to make the world cancer-free. I just noticed that the fight has over time claimed too much of me, and believe me, just like St. Paul in the Holy Bible, your daughter is down to the last drop!"

Life can sometimes prove so cruel, disastrous, and unbearable. However, many individuals have attained huge breakthroughs during such moments. It is all about knowing how to blossom amid a disaster, especially for Caroline and her family, who knew and believed God in heaven. All they needed to do was pray trustingly and wait, nothing more. One thing at a time. As a man in the movies, the Quiet Man says, "When I drink whisky, I drink whisky; and when I drink water, I drink water." Though facing the darkest moments of their lives, they had to understand the hour. It was the darkest hour; the last hour of the night and daytime would be forthcoming. Caroline was back at her feet again. She vowed not to mourn anymore, to try her best, and leave a legacy for her late daughter. The time was ripe for her to try some other path. Leynah's note signaled the end of the long night. The river was not yet dry. She (Caroline) was the source, and she had remained with a single stream which, if well-guarded, could blossom.

"If you are walking along and you find your path leading nowhere, then it is only wise to try some other path." 'The River and the Source: -Margaret A. Ogola

"I've been as low as anybody can go, and as high as anyone can go and you can always overcome these problems that one may have." - Tyson Fury

-GIDEON A. MUTAI-

Nairobi, Kenya.

Gideon A. Mutai is a final year undergraduate student at The Technical University of Kenya pursuing a bachelor's degree in Surveying Technology. He doubles up as a passionate poet, researcher, and storyteller. Since his early years in school, he knew he loved writing. Currently, he is on the verge of advancing his writing skills to reach greater heights and inspire humanity, just like how the world's renowned writers do daily.

Instagram:
@stories_of_our_lifetime

"BREAKING BOUNDARIES"

Growing up years

As a child, I was always fearful. Back then, I was not able to pinpoint exactly what I was scared of. But as I grew older, I recognised the trigger points that I am fearful of new people, new things and new situations.

I was not the easiest kid to take care of as I always had such fears that other kids do not have. And because I was so young, I did not know the way to recognise and regulate my fear / anxiety.

Bullying

It was not helpful too when every year (most of the time), our teachers and classmates change every school year. The sense of familiarity and a safe haven were being stripped down. It also did not help when some kids in school ostracised other kids too just because they look, think and behave differently from them.

"Everyone has a story to tell. Different doesn't mean weird, everyone is unique. So don't lose your sparks because of that."
-Bethany, 2022.

Looking back, the kids who ostracised others probably wanted to either have fun or they felt insecure or inferior. They are still finding their sense of identity - who they are and what they are good at.

Others then join the bullies as they are seen as a "stronger" community and bully others just not to go against the bullies. This then results in a herd mentality and those who suffered are those who refused to go against the norms and the weaker one whose voices were not being heard. There is this imbalance within them which reminds me of this quote -

"All of humanity's problems stem from man's inability to sit quietly in a room alone." -Blaise Pascal, 1600

We always like to think we are the triggers to someone else's reactions.

Personal encounters

Most of my school life from primary to secondary school, I have been ostracised or being in a "not so cool" group. I think I was a little unlucky as I was from one of the elite primary schools in Singapore. Hence people there were mostly rich and gifted. Whereas I am just an average Singaporean girl with average looks and intelligence. But because I was in that community, that comparison gap became larger and it seems that everything about me was bad when it is not necessarily true.

There were two particular instances which I remembered until now. First instance happened in Primary One when I was awarded the "Best Pupil Award". On that day, I was surprised and happy that many of my classmates wanted to eat recess with me and even gave me presents! As normally, I would spend recess alone outside my classroom. Please pardon me, it might seem like a small thing but as a child back then, it means everything. I was so surprised and confused. But that did not last long. Within the next few days, life was back to normal and back then, I do not have an explanation on why they actually bothered to do what they did. I would rather them not to do anything as at one moment, they sent me straight to heaven and the next moment, back to earth. I am also not sure if I should conclude to say that it was transactional as they only found me in my good days but regardless of which, it doesn't matter anymore.

Another occasion was in Primary Three where I wanted to tag along with two girls for recess but they did not want me to join. They did not tell me directly and went to hide in one of the toilets near our classroom. I had to chase them and bang on their toilet doors. They refused to come out and acted like they were not inside. Back then, I felt helpless and disappointed.

Looking back, it is not that I am so caught up with wanting someone to eat with me during recess but the fact that I simply do not understand and I have no explanation what I did "wrong" to be treated like an outcast. I just wanted to have a sense of belonging in the community that I was in.

It was a real struggle to cope with all this unnecessary negativity and to find a sense of belonging and my own identity. It was hard to see the light at the end of the tunnel!

And all these childhood traumas, it is not easy to recognise and understand. For example, some of my friends fear to eat alone in public even as an adult. Sometimes, it is not the act of eating alone in public that is scary but our personal experiences that ties to eating alone. It can be due to one individual's past. These traumas do have a spill over effect to adulthood and trigger other situations in life too. And one needs to be patient and trust themselves that they will rise above these things and will soon come to pass.

Moving on to secondary school, life was also similar to primary school but this time round - bullying was towards the indirect ways. Due to this, I thought that my whole life will probably be like this. I always prayed to have good friends and to have a strong social support group.

Turning Point

It was only when I was 16 where I entered pre-university (polytechnic) where I found my own tribe and really started having fun with friends. Likewise in university as well, I am not sure if it is puberty that is doing the job that turned the ugly duckling to a more normal duckling.

Count your blessings, least one forgets!" -Bethany, 2022.

"Though no one can go back and make a brand-new start, anyone can start from now and make a brand-new ending. - Carl Bard, n.d."

Intentional Parenting

As young children, it is hard to verbalise how they are feeling and what they should do next at times. Hence, parents have an important role to mitigate the impact on this.

As mentioned above, bullying tends to happen when people are feeling inferior about themselves and still finding out about themselves - what they are good at and what they are not.

This is where having hobbies come into play. Parents should expose their children to as many activities beyond academics like sports to performing arts. Not only do these activities allow children to know themselves better, it also provides them the platform for self-expression.

"Life is more than school. Life is more than the bullies. Likewise, once we enter adulthood, life is more than work. Life is more than the heartbreaks you had. Life is more than the failures you deemed it to be." -Bethany, 2022.

Adulting

I would like to share that school and life are two very different ball games. Yes, there is some truth where if you do well in school, you will have a good head start and it builds your confidence. Likewise, for those who have been struggling in school be it bullying or academically, this teaches one's resilience and empathy. If you are able to emerge through this, it trains your "resilience muscles" and you will be able to do it again and again with no sweat.

Schools will always like to categorise winners and losers. But life has not. In some schools, they will give you as many times as you want to get the right answer. But life bears no slightest resemblance to anything.

Breaking the cycle, breaking boundaries, champion mindset

Furthermore, I would like to share regarding what helped me through life in general and my bullying journey.

1. **Self-awareness → Choice → Mindset**

It is very important to first recognise and be careful with our feelings, thoughts, actions and intentions. And then choosing to manifest only those which work and cultivate to our highest good.

The only real asset we have is our mind where we have dominion over. Each of us has the CHOICE of what we want to put in our brain once we are old enough. We may not be in control of what happens in life but we are in control of our mind. Also, our inner self-talk makes all the difference between feeling a failure and making a success in your life.

2. **Past VS Present**

I think sometimes, one of the reasons why people find it hard to move forward and achieve more is due to them holding on to the past.

Focus on the present. Recognise that things that happen to and around us and emotions that come along with the situation are meant to be in the moment. They are temporary and will eventually pass. This brings you peace.

One of the reasons why we need to focus on the present is when we hold onto a thought and feelings, we are dragging it back from the past to the present and allowing something that has

ALREADY happened to affect us in the present. This does not allow us much room to move forward when we keep holding onto the past. Stay wise, do not bring unnecessary pain to yourself twice. Let go and embrace the present moment. The sooner we let go, the faster we heal.

Another reason why we need to focus on the present is because how we want our life to be is in our hands right now. It is not the future, it is not the past.

"Live and let live. If you have decided to move on, stay moved on. Whatever else happens, does not matter anymore." -Bethany, 2022.

On a good note, if you have taken the first step today, you have already changed your life. As this action means that you are willing to see your life change and you have already forged a single neural pathway. This makes it easier for you to do it again and increases the chances of producing a satisfying life. No goodness comes from worrying or feeling sorry for yourself. Stay in the light, keep positive, keep pushing on and things will turn good.

"Life is like riding a bicycle. To keep your balance, you must keep moving." -Albert Einstein

"Start by doing what is necessary, then do what's possible and suddenly you are doing the impossible." -Francis of Assisi, n.d.

3. Comparison and the right company

The second last portion that I want to share is about comparison and walking the journey with the right company. Don't compare yourself with others as everyone is unique and has their own path to walk. It will turn you bitter.

Also be intentional about your time and whom you spend it with. Remove negative influences from your life as negative thoughts and influences eventually become negative choices and actions.

"You will never reach your destination if you stop and throw stones at every dog that barks. Learning to ignore things is one of the great paths to inner peace."
-Winston S. Churchill, n.d

4. **Trust - Trust that journey ahead is a better one (by taking actions and when the stars are aligned)**

The last portion that I want to share is trust. Trust that the journey ahead is better than the one before. And this can only happen when we take actions and of course, a little luck is involved (which we have no control over so let's focus on taking actions). Take ownership of your actions and decisions!

"Your life does not get better by chance, It gets better by change. -Jim Rohn"

"Luck is what happens when preparation meets opportunity. - Seneca"

It is important to recognise that it is no one's responsibility to make you happy and no one owes you anything. You are the leader of your own life so stop giving up your power by expecting someone or something to change your life. As soon as you accept that, you take your power back and this makes you the most powerful person you can be.

"Be willing to do the uncomfortable work so that your future looks more like your future more than your past." -Bethany, 2022.

No one has it all figured out. Also, sometimes you would not get the answers to the things that hurt you the most. But I hope we all choose to forgive too as one day we will need to be forgiven too so learn to forgive others. And do ourselves a favour, if you care too much about others - you become their slave.

We will get there someday and we will live well.

Take good care of yourself and with love,
Beth.

-GOH JIA HUEY, BETHANY-

Singapore

This is Bethany, born and raised in a sunny island country called "Singapore". We are small but mighty and likewise, anyone who believes in themselves too - can be mighty.

She graduated from university back last year in 2021 where she studied "Human Resource with Psychology". Now she is doing Talent Acquisition in one of the largest crypto exchanges in the world. Adulting has been fun and crazy (scary with responsibilities) but she wanted to take some time off to write something close to her heart - mental health and in particular, bullying.

Before she moves on, she wants to take a moment to say thank you to you for being here and sharing your time and attention with her. She hopes that this little piece of the story could bring some hope and light during your darkest days.
And remember, limits are set by us and we can always break boundaries.

If you like what you read below, you can always find her on Instagram at *@gritandgracesg* where she posts daily quotes with a theme in mind. The story behind "gritandgracesg" is that she always believed in doing things intentionally and mental health should be a balance of taking actions (grit) and self-care (grace).

Lastly, thank you Chee San for believing in this dream of mine and being a part of @gritandgracesg. ***-Bethany.***
Take good care,
Beth.
Instagram: @gritandgracesg

"AFFIRMING GUIDE TO SELF-LOVE FROM SPARKFUL CREATIVE"

25 Positive Affirmations for When You Need Help with a Lift

If you need a boost of positivity, comfort, or hope, this list of affirmations is for you. Try reading them out loud or even saying them in front of a mirror.

1. I am wonderful just as I am.
2. I am thankful for who I am.
3. I can dream big dreams.
4. I am adored.
5. I am valued for who I am.
6. I am supported throughout my day.
7. I am at peace.
8. I am achieving my dreams.
9. I can take on anything that comes my way.
10. What I put my mind to I can achieve, I just need to believe.
11. I have the courage to take on anything.
12. My future is anything I create.
13. Success comes to me.
14. I am thriving.
15. I am a beautiful being.
16. Opportunities come to me.
17. My luck is limitless.
18. I live in peace with myself.
19. I have choices in my life.
20. I am open to receiving good gifts.
21. My life is open to unlimited opportunities.
22. I have the ability to decide what I do and do not want.
23. There is hope for me.
24. My future is bright.
25. I am creating a life I love.

Self-Compassion Affirmations

Treating yourself with grace and compassion should be done. Use these affirmations to guide yourself on a journey to be kinder and more compassionate to yourself.

I like to speak these affirmations out loud or during meditation. You can also print and tape these phrases to a mirror so that you see them every day.

1. I am thankful for my ability to be compassionate and loving.
2. I am free from other's judgements.
3. I honor my own choices.
4. I am reaching my dreams.
5. I take steps with courage.
6. I try my best and that is enough.
7. I respect myself for who I am.
8. I am safe living my truth.
9. I embrace the best parts of myself.
10. I take time for myself.
11. I choose to forgive myself.
12. I accept myself, I am true to me.
13. I give myself time to heal.
14. I embrace myself fully.
15. I am doing the best I can.
16. I am showing up for myself.
17. I am compassionate toward myself.
18. I try to be good enough just as I am.
19. I recognize the good in myself.
20. I cheer myself on.
21. I need to give myself the benefit of the doubt at the time.
22. I am gentle with myself.
23. The world is full of happiness and joy and I claim it for myself.
24. I am worthy of confidence.
25. I give myself over to love and joy.

"Write a Letter" Journaling Prompts

There are many emotions that we often need to express. Having an outlet to write a letter that is never sent can be a way to express those feeling and let your inner voice be heard. There is no judgement, because no postage is ever applied, just pure feelings.

- Dear me I'm thankful for you because…
- Dear younger self I have to tell you…
- Dear me I forgive you because…
- Dear person who inspired me…
- Dear person who gave me hope…
- Dear person who believed in me…
- Dear person who left me behind…
- Dear person who hurt my feelings…
- Dear person I want you to understand…
- Dear person who forgave me…
- Dear person I forgive you because…
- Dear person I need you to hear this…
- Dear person I'm ready to tell you…
- Dear person I love you…
- Dear person I miss you…

15 Ways to Practice Self Love

Embracing self-love is a journey. There are many ways to practice self-love, whether it be from your mind, body or soul. Follow this simple guide for ideas on how to refresh yourself with some self-loving.

Mind

1. Making a list of what you are grateful for in your life. Take some time to celebrate your life and the journey you've been on.
2. Spend time on the passions you love. If you love painting or playing tennis, do what you love. Make time for yourself and what you love.
3. Work toward your goals. Keep moving forward and making progress toward what you want to accomplish.
4. Practice self-compassion. Work toward being gentler, and kinder, with yourself. When you learn to be compassionate with yourself, it will overflow to others.
5. Celebrate your wins, any size. Take time to celebrate the journey of life and praise yourself along the way.

Body

1. Take the time to prepare a nourishing meal for your body. If you can, try using fresh fruits and vegetables.
2. Move your body. Find yourself in nature or watch an exercise video.
3. Cleanse yourself with a fresh shower and bath. Let the water flow over you and let it wash away your cares.
4. Wear clothes that make you feel good about you. Embrace what feels good to your body and wear what you love. You are the only opinion that counts when it comes to your clothes.

5. Be mindful of your body. Tune into what your body is saying; listen and learn. Be aware of your needs and be ready to serve them.

Soul

1. You can try repeating affirmations to yourself. Make a list of your favorite affirmations and try saying them either to yourself in front of a mirror.
2. Try meditation. Spend ten minutes either meditating to yourself or with a guided meditation. Try downloading the app “Insight Timer” for easy meditations.
3. Try to release relationships that no longer serve you. Work to build a community that is full of love and acceptance. Make room in your life for people that build you up. If you can, work to let go of people that do not.
4. Make a list of what you love about yourself. Make the effort you appreciate yourself and all that you are.
5. Unplug for some time. Let yourself have time to breathe, and let go of tech for a day.

-JESSIE BRITO-

California, United States of America.

Jessie Brito is a daydreamer, glass half-full, hopeful romantic. They love bringing inspiration to others and helping others achieve their best. Their dream is to help others love themselves more, talk kinder to themselves, and spread love to those around them. Excerpts were taken from their website. For more, visit their website.

Website: SparkfulCreative.com

Instagram @sparkfulcreative

"REFLECTIONS"

Broken

This short poem denotes the trauma, confusion and complexities of a person with an afflicted mind.

Regularly irregular…absolutely brazen!
The livid thoughts of an afflicted mind,
Absolutely odd, outlandish…driving others to the corner
You can feel the trembling waves,
Yes, it comes in waves…waves of
Incorrigible, unaccountable rage and nonsense.

Shaking the very foundation of beings around…
Rocking across borders of affected terrains,
Trembling like the aftermath of an earthquake,
Eyes look- shimmering with cruelty…
A soul lost in the maze of its own confusions,
Stammering, fumbling, blabbering, chattering.

Searching for lost comfort- everywhere
Finding none, anywhere…
Blackhole of a mind, filled with terror and loneliness,
Hanging on to people, cruelly thwarting their minds…
Stratums of absurd, panic-stricken thoughts',
Matured by the bubbling elixir of fantasy.

Turning and shifting, trying to sort out
The never-ending crisis of life…
Ah! What a burden it must be,
A life of an afflicted mind…
Unaware of what to do- swimming in darkness of time,
Till eternity calls you again
Into its cradle of everlasting joy

And provides restoration and glory,
To take a better shape next time.

Metamorphosis

This poem is about the recovery journey of an individual who was tormented by a toxic parent, the difficulties in pulling oneself up and creating the change.

Encircling darkness of self-denial
Years of voices that threw the cruel slanders
Creating monstrous emotional abyss
A herculean task, to recover from…
That continuous flow of negativity
Which tore the soul apart…?

But, no, don't give up, said a voice from behind
It's time for metamorphosis- a complete one that too!
Life is not only black and dreadful
Not everybody is harrowing or heinous
Cast off the shadows of despondency
Created in you, most ominously,
Said that gentle, guiding voice…
For its time for metamorphosis- a complete one that too!

The elixir of life is all yours
It fell on her like an epiphany
To feel the felicity of life,
In all its beauty and joy, the self-realisation-
The understanding, the ineffable joy of comely confidence.

Slowly she was becoming sure, of herself-
As a person, as a human…
Yes, that's how we go about it lil one'
Said that gentle, but persuasive voice
This is the metamorphosis we've been waiting for.

The End

This poem is dedicated to all the lonely people, who are overwhelmed by the lack of empathy and loneliness, they face in the world today.

The world is not a place for
People like you and me –
Who do not understand cruelty,
Unknown are the ways of vile villains
Who lurks around the corners –
Waiting for the right time and opportunity
To pounce upon its prey –

You never know what hit you?!
Was it thunder… or some bolt out of the blue?
Till you realize your blunder
And how amused is the predator!
Watching the victim pulsating in pain.
The aftermath of which may take eons to recover,
And the scars of which would never fade.

Pretensions, absurdity, nonchalant atrocity
In extreme totality, destroying
Your emotions, stamping all feelings to dust.
Oh, it is, as if you were some mere pieces of rotten meat.

Heartless insanity shown towards a being!
After all, aren't innocent souls worth anything?
Yes, to exist in this present world;
One has to be insane!
Move on like zombies with your tattered souls
Or-react, my lord! You need redemption!
Or start being like them – inhuman,
Cruel – emotionless – pathetic!

It's easier said than done – so
I guess dear one, it would be
Better to follow your way –
Leave this mad house and go away
Never to return –
To this endlessly cruel world.
K. Kavikkal (Pen name)

-KEERTHI VARMA-

Kerala, India.

Keerthi Varma, born in Kerala, India is a teacher, education professional and an academic head who specializes in English Language and Literature. Throughout her 20-year-plus spanning career, she has had the chance to meet and mingle with a variety of people including children and adults. Although she worked in the education industry, her passion for writing was innate right from childhood. Here she has penned down from her heart her perspectives on different angles of the human psyche, thus bringing her passion for writing into realization. Though her pre-university and post-graduation are in English literature, her graduation was in psychology, due to her immense interest in the subject.

Above are a few notes that explore the different shades of the human mind in her humble understanding. Each refers to distinct areas, as observed by her, put into words to capture its essence.

Email: **keerthimurali63@gmail.com**
LinkedIn: Keerthi Murali

"MENTAL HEALTH AND THE SOCIETY"

I WANT TO START MY PART WITH A FEW QUESTIONS!

HOW COMFORTABLE ARE YOU WITH SHARING YOUR MENTAL HEALTH ISSUES WITH THE FAMILY OR SOCIETY?

HOW OFTEN DO YOU THINK ABOUT BEING JUDGED?

WHAT MATTERS TO YOU THE MOST?
The likes on social media or your actual well-being.

Recall The Last time you had a deep conversation with your parents or grandparents!!!

In today's era, we worry more about likes and comments on Instagram rather than our smiles or someone else's happiness.

Recall the last time you had a walk at a park without any gadgets.

The last time you felt connected with nature by the means of your eyes, not by the lens of the camera.

We can find a glimpse of anxiety within many people around us, but nobody discusses it. They just pretend that everything is alright!!!

The Last Conversation

CHARACTERS OF THE STORY

JENNIFER: THE GRANDMOTHER
LUCY: GRANDDAUGHTER
ELENA; MOTHER
JACOB: FATHER
ERIC: GRANDSON

It's a usual Monday morning,
Elena is preparing breakfast,
Jacob is getting ready to leave for the office
and the kids are getting ready to go to school,

Jennifer asked Lucy “IS EVERYTHING ALRIGHT?”

Lucy replied,
“ALL OK GRANNY!”

But granny understood that something was not well.
This keeps bothering granny the whole day.

When Lucy returned home from school,
She went to the room straight away.

For the past few months, Lucy was not having the usual conversations with the family,
she would usually stay busy on her phone most of the time.

But this time, things were different as she wanted to say something but she couldn’t, maybe the gap was restraining her from saying something.

Granny was very sad that night, she wrote a beautiful poem for her granddaughter to make her comfortable.

I don’t want money,
I want the smile of my honey.
I don’t want much of your time,
just a cute smile.
I don’t ask for emojis,
I am happy with your expressions.
I don’t ask for gifts,
you're the best gift I have.
I want my Lucy back.
SADLY, the granny died that night!

The whole family was in sorrow.
Eric found this poem under granny’s pillow and
gave it to LUCY.
Lucy started crying the moment she saw the poem.
Then she shared her worries with her parents,
she felt relaxed after.

She was in a state of depression due to mental trauma caused by her boyfriend,
but she couldn’t say it to anyone.

Sadly, granny died without having a conversation with Lucy!

The last conversation they had was,
“ALL OK GRANNY!”

We stay together under one roof,
but do we stay together?

Do we have a mutual understanding?
Does living together implies understanding?
Physical presence is important but what about mental presence?
Lack of communication is one of the most common causes of mental health deterioration.

At times we keep thinking about the reaction of others.

In today's era, there is a clear-cut demarcation between parents and children.

I don't blame social media for this!
It's us who are more worried about likes than a smile!

It's us who are more influenced by the FAKE than the REAL!
It's us who keep checking the messages continuously rather than checking up on our mental well-being!
Moments can be captured in reels, but life can be summed up by the real ones only!

Social media is a selective platform,
It should be us, to use it wisely!

THE END

~Khan Hussain Alig

-KHAN HUSSAIN ALIG-

Karnataka, India.

Hussain is a medical student from India who loves to write. He started his journey of writing as a poet. He prefers writing romantic poetry. His inspiration comes from Mirza Ghalib. The writer has previously performed in many open mic events as a poet. This is the first time he's written on mental health, it was a great experience for him. Hopefully, you all will enjoy my piece, "he states".

Email: ceomycitydoctors@gmail.com
Instagram: @khanalighussain

LinkedIn: Hussain Khan

"UNREVEALED SECRET TO A BETTER LIVING"

(Originally posted on April 26, 2022, on my blog https://khushnnum.com)

I've always been a little too emotional and sensitive. But, if you are reading this, you too are looking out to discover the unrevealed secret to a better living.

However, as I grew older, I realized how important emotions are. When we neglect or ignore them, it becomes a tipping point that gives birth to grave issues such as shame, vulnerability, abandonment, compassion, empathy, and a lack of connection with ourselves and others.

Emotional awareness allows us to understand and experience what we want and don't want. It isn't just limited to objects or things; that's just the tip of the iceberg; it goes deeper than our minds comprehend. Life transforms if we all begin to accept, look within, and engage in self-work.

The unrevealed secret to a better living boils down to our very emotions and how we handle them.

People are ashamed of accepting it. Therefore, it isn't easy to express and address them. However, emotional awareness contributes to the quotient of attention that helps establish healthy relationships with everyone. This is because it allows us to talk about our feelings more openly, keeps us away from unresolved conflicts, and helps to express our self-difficult feelings with ease.

The Five Fundamental Emotions and Their Impact on Our Overall Well-being

There are various emotions, and we will go over each one in greater detail, interestingly, how these emotions influence our daily lives by providing us with first-hand experience with either positive or negative outcomes. Emotions influence our overall behaviour and how we live and interact with others.

The decisions we make, the actions we take, and the perceptions we hold are all influenced by the emotions we are experiencing at the time.

1) Happiness

"HAPPINESS" is the most loved, cherished, and desired emotion that we will be discussing in greater depth. We run from pillar to post to experience and have this in our lives. Happiness is commonly defined as a pleasurable state signified by feelings of contentment, joy, gratitude, and overall comfort.

Since the 1960s, there has been a significant increase in intrinsic exploration and analysis in many fields, including psychology and human behaviour. Positive psychology is the name given to this branch of psychology. There isn't just one way to express this emotion; here are a few examples of how we do so when we feel the most desirable emotion.

- A warm smile.
- Going out of our way to appreciate and complement our loved ones.
- Going above and beyond to help someone
- Being more relaxed.
- Feeling more energized and grounded.
- Feeling calm, excited, and more focused.

2) Sadness

Sadness is another important emotion that is ephemeral. It pervades feelings such as discomfort, rage, helplessness, suppression, and sorrow.

This is an emotion that we all experience at times. In some cases, extended and acute sadness can lead to depression. Sadness can be expressed in a variety of forms.

- Frustration
- Anger

- Shouts and screams
- Going Silent
- Self-Denial
- Self-Withdrawal

The complexity and depth of sadness can vary depending on the primary cause, and how people deal with this emotion is also essential.

Sadness can cause people to engage in stress adaptation. For example, it could be taking too many medications, excessive drugs, disconnecting from everyone, and avoiding being vocal. Doing so can aggravate feelings of sadness and lengthen the time it takes to recover from the same.

3) Fear

What feelings does fear elicit in you? Aside from physical symptoms, people experience mental and behavioural symptoms such as extreme vulnerability, overwhelming, feeling lost and confused, feeling disconnected, and a sense of being close to death.

Fear is a powerful emotion that causes people to flee or fight.

Fear is our perception of a situation and how we react to it. Fear is an acronym that stands for "False Evidence Appearing Real."

Fear affects everyone differently. Some people are overly sensitive, and they are more likely to experience this emotion instantly.

Physical:

- Excessive Sweating
- Hands or feet trembling
- Suffering from suffocation
- Inability to express
- Feeling disoriented

Mental:

- Agitation
- Anxiety
- Panic

Emotional:

- Constant bursts of tears
- Disconnected feelings
- Unable to put your trust in anyone

4) Anger

Anger is one of the most common emotions, and we all express this in some or the other way. It induces bitterness, disquiet, annoyance, and antipathy towards others.

It is commonly thought to be a negative emotion; however, it can also be productive and helpful in gaining clarity or setting boundaries in relationships. In addition, it points you in the direction of taking action on issues that are bothering you.

Anger can cause problems if expressed excessively or insufficiently, harmful to oneself and others. In addition, anger without boundaries can lead to adverse outcomes such as hostility, brutality, and cruelty.

5) Surprise

A surprise is the least common of the five emotions. It refers to a mental and emotional reaction to something unexpected.

This emotion can be optimistic, pessimistic, or neutral, depending on the circumstances.

We will feel enormous joy and pleasure when surprised by something optimistic in nature.

On the other hand, when pessimistic, our feelings will be more akin to powerlessness, anger, and shattered.

The feeling of neutrality is defined as feeling nothing in particular.

Conclusion

We've just learned about five basic emotions and how they influence our daily lives.

The significance of accepting it and the adverse effects it may have on our overall well-being if we do not.
Let's go over how to spot them and deal with them so we can release the pent-up energy.

10 practical steps for dealing with emotions-
We'll focus on a single emotion in this segment to help you understand how to cope with it in small steps.

We must all deal with it somehow; it helps to calm us down and bring our feelings and pent-up energy caused by emotional turmoil to the surface.

Take a few moments to walk through the next ten steps mentally. Then, if necessary, close your eyes.

Step 1:
Take note of your current emotion and how is it affecting you.
Your Current Emotion:

Step 2:
Examine the emotion in its current state. How does it make you feel? Look at it without judgment
Your Current Emotion:

Step 3:
Recall that emotion and ask yourself if it has anything to do with your reality. If you observe it without judgment, it has nothing to do with your ongoing issue. All of our pain and suffering arise when we become overly critical and judgmental.
Your Current Emotion:

Step 4:
Consider what you can glean from that emotion. What is it trying to tell you, and how can you use it to help you progress?
Your Current Emotion:

Step 5:
Please pay close attention to how that emotion shaped all of your experiences, possibly leading you to agree you'll never get out of it.
Your Current Emotion:

Step 6:
Recall why you felt compelled to associate with this emotion and the story accompanying it. Then, consider the possibility that you could have separated yourself from it.
Your Current Emotion:

Step 7:
Recall how this emotion manifested itself, and write down your thoughts on how it hampered your potential.
Your Current Emotion:

Step 8:
Take note of how you were attracting more unfavourable outcomes associated with this emotion.
Your Current Emotion:

Step 9:
Consider how you made mental suffering out of that emotion by infusing it with your perception.
Your Current Emotion:

Step 10:
Eventually, you'll realize that your emotion was only a mental construct, and you'll notice that your reality is unaffected.
Your Current Emotion:
Post Tags: #emotions #vulnerability #wayoflife #wholeheartedliving

-KHUSHNUM K SIDHVA-

**Mumbai, India.**

This here is Khushnum Sidhva, she is an entrepreneur, a working professional and an upcoming writer.

Since the 2020 pandemic, she came across her talent and creativity where she stepped into making "Designer Handmade Bath and Body Care Hampers" and with that it has given her an overwhelming response ever since revolving her art and creativity.

She also discovered that writing is being creative and through all her learnings and exposures she has currently stepped into the world of writing.

She doesn't know where and what the journey lies ahead for her, but she knows the Universe has always guided her perfectly to the place where she should be.

LinkedIn: Khushnum Sidhva
Email: khushnumsidhva@gmail.com
Instagram: @natureandyou7

"STUCK WITH A NARCISSIST"

Dear Diary,

It feels like the sun has set, darkness arose and happiness is out of sight. I can see myself turning from a leaded wall to shattered pieces, my fortunes have turned into unfortunates. My reign has come to its end. I lost my dream job, the job that took me fifteen years and costed me an arm and a leg. I dearly paid for every ounce of it, being pronounced as Dr. Neil Browne was so blissful. And now just in a flick, it's all gone. I saw smiles on faces for I was holding the knife. I've experienced the miracle of nature and now I wonder when will one happen to me. Maybe it would have been easier for me to go through this time when my faith is fading. Alas, I am not even worthy of love. The only woman who walked through my heart, her angelic eyes bought peace to me, her nubile beauty was harmony to me, her presence was melancholic, she was my only empathy, love of my life, Julien. Soon she became popcorn to my movie, wrapper to my candy, water for my rivers, happiness to my festival, we were perfect together.

As they say, love is tragic, the blooming garden started to die and the ocean that was calm turned into a hurricane washing away all love. I thought that it would be nice to introduce Julien to my friends I invited my best friend Ron and Emma for dinner, they have been happily married for three years. I thought that it would be amazing for all four of us, we will hang out together, make memories together, we will be like a college friends' group. Unfortunately, that wish remained just a wish. The moment Emma and Ron entered the restaurant Julien made fun of Emma's dress saying that it was cheap and outdated, Emma was discomposed. Emma baked us some cookies as a gesture of love, Julien claimed them as disgusting. After the dinner it was time to pay the bill, I was supposed to pay the bill because it was my treat but, Julien handed over the cheque to Ron knowing the fact that he couldn't afford it. It was all very embarrassing for me, while driving back home I told Julien that what she did was wrong, answering me back she said, that I should be grateful for I have such a beautiful wife even though I'm black.

To the mankind,
Who is kind,
To all shapes, all shades,
With no hate.

All shades are beautiful I thought, but Julien made me feel inferior to her as if I'm not even a human, as if I'm not worthy enough for love, she wasn't even sorry for it. I was flabbergasted, but that wasn't it, her bossy character heightened every day. She sold my bike that I bought in college and bought a piece of jewellery instead claiming that buying bikes is a waste of money. I made so many memories in my youth with that bike and now it was someone else's. She enrolled me in a gym so that I can work out and build a good physique. I expressed my wish of not going to the gym, she got upset left the house and told me that she felt embarrassed to introduce me to her friends because I was fat and black and that she was fair and white. According to her, we were not even a good couple. I was made a victim of both racism and body shaming. Moreover, when my colleague David got promoted to the chief of department, she insulted me, taunted me for I couldn't get the promotion. she made fun of me and reminded me how lucky I am for I have her as my wife, even though I'm black and fat. That wasn't enough, my father was not well and he couldn't do any job to pay the bills, so I decided that I would support him financially but Julien didn't just let me do it. I couldn't meet my parents, my family, I couldn't even attend any family dinner, now I was all alone just surrounded by Julianne and nobody else. No friends no family!

It sets me secluded,
Now I'm on a feud.
I've set all ties to die,
For a new life I comply.

Read the full poem @words_of_reality6 on Instagram.

It's easier to walk away but it's difficult to detach from it, mentally and emotionally. It requires guts to walk out especially when one doesn't know its worth. I made a decision that I don't want to live in such a toxic relationship, thus I applied for a divorce paper. I had those divorce papers in my drawer for months, every morning I would think that today I will tell Julian about it and I will end all this, but every moment made was confusing and scary, that if I lose her I will lose everything else in my life and I wasn't understanding the fact that because of her I have already lost everything in my life .One morning I gathered some cottage and handed over the divorce paper to Julian the love inside me thought to give her a second chance, instead of trying to fix things between us, Julien made stories of torture and abuse to tell the people, to show the world that how bad I am as a husband and as a human, it was getting more difficult for me to get out of this relationship Julien gained sympathy of our common people and everyone was trying to explain to me that how bad I was. The world didn't know the other side of the story, the world didn't know my state of mind. Ignoring every opinion, I chose to walk out and I did.

The wind that blows,
brings along new hope.
The sand you walk on,
speaks the sense of bloom.
The sky is pink,
future to be linked.
The ocean is will,
the gushes will sink.

I shifted from that city to a completely new city where I could start over everything, my parents moved in with me and they stood firmly to support me. I learned a lesson that day, a home is a home no matter how late you return. My parents love me the same as they did before I got married to Julian now, I had a very big responsibility to rebuild my relationship with my parents and to start living my dream job once again. Gradually, I was becoming a better version of myself, I started to speak publicly about narcissism, racism and bad relationships, it got me fame and slowly people started to resonate with me, and my thoughts were loved by people. I was invited on TV channels to talk about medicine and about my personal story, the sun that had once faded was lighting up again and again and I learned that every time you fall it's your responsibility to rise back, there's always power in the nature that supports you, that brings hope to you, but the first step must be taken by your own self. The world can support us but we must learn how to walk on our own. A bad relationship made me feel why me? but today I am thankful that it was me! Because today I have a bucket full of lessons that taught me that the first form of love is self-love. No matter what happens in your life one should never question its worth.

Racism is raised like a child

When an embryo formed
We nourish it
With hate and anger
A heart formed
With no love
For the weeping eyes.

When it first spoke with grudge
We braced it to strengthen
And whites blustered
Over the black's blisters
They felt suffocated
And the child heightens.

-MAHAM SHAIKH-

Karachi, Pakistan.

Maham Shaikh, is a pre-medical student for A-levels. Teenage has been very rough on her, she states. To stand tall she took the support of words and indeed words are most powerful. Stories are like mirrors, they reflect the reality of life and happiness is in living the reality. She's going astray to the people where words and skills are more important than money and fame.

She was someone who has experienced narcissism on her own thus she feels the importance of being independent both mentally and financially. This search for freedom from toxic relationships has got her into the art of writing.

Instagram: @words_of_reality6

Email: mahamfawadshaikh@gmail.com

Twitter: @moontheshykh

"INTERROGATING WOMEN'S MENTAL HEALTH DURING THE LOCKED DOWN INDIA: A BRIEF DISCUSSION"

The world witnessed the most unexpected disaster when Covid-19 was declared a pandemic on 11th of March, 2020. People not only suffered physically and emotionally, but also faced huge financial losses due to this deadly virus. An uncountable number of lives were lost and the entire world went under lockdown. This resulted in a hike in mental health issues amongst people of every age. The masses have suffered through and through at the hands of a deadly virus that shook not only the backbone of functionality but also highlighted prevalent mental health issues that mask inside the household setting. This discussion will be, however, regarding women and their mental health during the pandemic in the context of Indian culture. This essay aims at critically engaging with the issue, in terms of not data analysis but more in the sense of questioning the politics behind the problem.

India is a nation of vast cultural practices and norms, which are sometimes inherently patriarchal in nature. From my own personal experiences as a woman hailing from a semi-urban space, it's not a surprise because women are so casually associated with housework and caretaking. The pandemic and lockdown certainly played a crucial part in highlighting the larger picture in Indian household settings where women had to work, more than ever, to provide, nurture and take care of their family during the time when hygiene was being considered as most important. Women who were already a part of the domestic sphere earlier would have their personal space after their counterparts left for work, but during the pandemic, even that space was taken away. President of the Indian Psychiatric Society Dr.N.N. Raju pointed out that whether people prefer to hear it or not, women perform the majority of the home chores. They were managing a number of fronts, including their workload, the children's online lessons, and the husband's requirements as he was operating from home during the outbreak[32]. This seems one of the major reasons for mental health issues amongst women. The lack of any personal space is a real issue that women in India face, especially the ones who are "homemakers". According to a study conducted by an economics professor at King's College London, women reported lower overall mental health than males across all mental stress aspects. In the second wave, reported mental stress was still significantly influenced by financial instability, again more so for women than for males[33]. Financial instability, thus, played a key factor in the deterioration of mental health amongst women in a society where gender pay disparity is already a huge issue.

Young women like me and many others, migrate from their small hometowns in order to pursue quality education and freedom of expression of personal identity. During the pandemic when all the educational institutes and hostels were closed, college students had no other option but to return to the safe space of their homes. But is home really a safe space for women who wish to live on their own terms? Well, the answer to this is simple and brutal as many of my fellow ladies shared similar narratives regarding how their mental health deteriorated during the pandemic when they were locked in their homes. They were not

[32] Bajeli-Datt, Kavita. "COVID-19 Spiked Women's Mental Health Woes in India, Say Studies- The New Indian Express." The New Indian Express, 12 Sept. 2022, www.newindianexpress.com/nation/2022/mar/12/covid-19-spiked-womens-mental-health-woes-in-india-say-studies-2429167.html.

only forced to do household chores without their will but were also hindered from expressing themselves. Many were policed regarding their clothes, many faced issues of privacy where their activities were monitored throughout the day while many were (Trigger warning) abused by their family members when they resisted the policing. In a private survey that I conducted for this essay, the result was that due to these inflictions on women, a rise in major breakdowns, depressive episodes and other mental health disorders occurred amongst most college-going women, especially the ones who hailed from developing areas in the country.

Indian Culture at large expects women to behave and be in a certain fashion. The flag holders of culture are mostly patriarchs who are deep-rooted in their notion of how a woman should act. It's important to acknowledge the role structural violence and patriarchy played in deteriorating the mental health of women at large. Women are expected to cater to the tantrums thrown by men of the household and the culture in a larger picture. These issues definitely got highlighted during the pandemic when the space to exercise freedom of expression of identity was taken away from women. The resultant hike in mental health issues amongst women is surely not a surprise as one of the critical causes of mental health issues emerges from home, when there is constant surveillance, policing, expectations and resistance.

[1] Roy, Sanchari. "Mental Health Crisis Deepened in India during COVID-19, Especially for Women | Feature from King's College London." Mental Health Crisis Deepened in India during COVID-19, Especially for Women | Feature from King's College London, 9 May 2022, www.kcl.ac.uk/mental-health-crisis-deepened-in-india-during-devastating-second-wave-especially-for-women.

-MANSI MISHRA-

Bangalore, India.

This here is Mansi, her pronouns are she/they and she is currently pursuing her Master's in English and Cultural Studies. Her areas of interest are gender studies, queer studies, postcolonial studies and comparative literature. She loves to write about contemporary issues and she is a big fan of "Ishmat Chugtai." "Her writings are a huge inspiration to me", she states.

"Hoping to contribute my best to the academia!"

Mansi Mishra

Instagram: @meownsiiii

Email: mansimishra0025@gmail.com

LinkedIn: Mansi Mishra

Website: twelvepointsomething.wordpress.com/

"FIRST LESSON"

Chapter-1

I woke up a little early today and just upon opening my eyes I felt like as if I was awake since eon and yet felt spirited with the sunshine hiding behind the curtains of my window until I sought it out and made the rest of my room filled with its shine. I got myself assembled maybe even before it is quarter past 6 of these winter mornings. The weather is bit clear this morning and birds were already sitting next to my calathea pot. I glanced out of the window and the street was filled with no people around. Then I took my regular walk through the park and fed the puppies as usual on my way back home, people and the sky both were as usual shining bright and were unheeded of the fact that today is going to be my first day at the medical school.

Last month I got selected for this medical school and I was festal since then.

I mean.. Why not?

After all, I prepared myself really hard and cleared the entrance with ample of marks. I've been really naive when I made this sane decision to be a medical doctor and help those whom I find suffering.

Because suffering is what I am most scared of...For me, suffering is the least desirable of any man-made emotion for any lively creature to feel. Suffering is the biggest of the curse amongst all the curses, suffering can change the blissful garden of roses into a barren land filled with thorns. It can change a person in and out. Suffering comes in cycles of tears and stays...yes! It might never go, only some could heal with the remedy of time. Suffering is the demon waiting to ominous the lives of innocents. When a person suffers, he never suffers alone...with him, all those he once touched in their hearts, suffers. Yet suffering perhaps turmoil the sanity of love. Suffering could leave you empty, it has this power to light your bridges of hope onto which you could never walk on, suffering is a dark room with no source of light and you are locked inside, alone...

After all these years of seeing people suffering around me, I've been always scared of this plethoric wave of sadness that comes with a face of suffering as it left you with no hope and glee.

Maybe that has been the reason why I always put myself pugnacious to rescue people in suffering, Also, this could be the only reason why I happen to be a doctor to save lives of hundreds from suffering, as if God has purposefully given me this ability in life to rescue people from their pain.

Taking a sip from my sipper, I looked at the calories I just burnt after walking and..

What!? It's 6:30 am!!

Now I am running late to be present on the first day of the class. I am so excited to leave my older self behind and be the newer version of me with this never returning turning point of my life. From today, I am going to learn to minimize the hardships of people suffering from illness and just by that maybe I would be able to find my remedy as well. Wish me the best of luck.☺

Chapter-2

I left for college at 7 as I can't take the risk to miss any of the happening today at the college.

"Dad, we're late already!" and I asked him to drive faster. Now I am just waiting to be at my college next.

I remember as I entered college with the best of my feelings and some ambitions that day, I was feeling so excited and yet nervous to meet the profound doctors of their field and learn medical science from them. While showing our ID's through the main gate, I was sitting by the window in the backseat and was trying my best to capture as much of the picture in my head as possible. I was trying to captivate all the visuals of the college because this was my first time at my dream place, I could see the beautiful red building standing aside from the phenomenal garden carrying colours of flowers, just as we left the main gate and moved ahead and passed the garden a beautiful fragrance from there ran out to my car as it was there to welcome all these people visiting the place, or if it tries to diminish one's suffering and that reached my heart directly. It definitely didn't feel like a hospital to me, it was a feeling of a homeland for sure, I took the fragrance in my heart and smiled back at the garden and this way I absquatulate the place and in return, I felt welcomed.

As my car moved ahead, I noticed a few people roaming in the garden wearing scrub suits, they were calm and healing. My car then took a right turn and now I can see a beautiful tall building covered in white paint and holding this board saying "MEDICAL COLLEGE". I instantly smiled and was looking out of the window as if I was a 5-year-old girl who was the happiest at the moment to look at her favourite place.

As soon I ingress the building I saw so many students of my age wearing apron rushing here and there in nervousness, it was the moment when we were asked to move towards the lecture theatre where we would be sitting for now and for the rest of the year. We stampede through the door of the lecture theatre and took a seat randomly. I found sitting in the 2nd last row and my adjacent vacant seat gave a little relief to put my bag onto it and I also doffed off my shrug to it. I opened my book and started reading the anatomy out of my avidity.

After a while, a gentleman of around 50 years in age with a 6ft tall component sparkling with his white hairs tangled in a male bun, sashayed into the theatre along with his ground touching brown long coat. He made his hand rest after putting his briefcase on the front table of the theatre. And I along with others stood for him to pay respect. He then with a loud voice began.

"Welcome to "INTERNATIONAL MEDICAL COLLEGE, INDIA" from today onwards, you'll be recognised as a medical student from one of the most impassable and esoteric places of graduation in the field of medical science with hundreds of eminent alumni waiting to teach you the best medical science

through their respective fields, this is your Dean and Professor, Dr. Alok Awasthi, I will be...."
May I come in sir!? (Someone asked through panting)

Chapter-3

A boy of my age group panting with a smile and face nearly red was standing at the door of the lecture theatre. His eyes were half covered with his hairs, a dimple on the cheek conterminous to his smile which was above his beard was perhaps looking cute. His hairs were all messy and his blue denim shirt was drenched in sweat, his eyes were the brightest amongst all those who had been present there, that too was guarded by a layer of round spectacles, his left shoulder was carrying the bag and overall, his presence was making some difference in the flux of the class.
May I come in sir!? He asked through his dimple smile and sweats with panting.
"Please enter", the professor replied.

"You can find your seat in the back of the class, ask someone to help you find it", The boy was guided by the professor.

"Thank you sir," he replied and headed towards the back of the theatre where all other seats were occupied, I noticed it. So, I suddenly took my bag from the adjacent corner seat and made it available for him to join. He was looking 360 degrees around the class for a seat and while looking for it, he missed my visuals and continued searching on the contrary row. As expected, the seats were all taken and then he continued his hunt, started moving his neck around the class for a seat again and this time even before when his eyes were reaching towards my row to look for a seat, I raised my hand and guided him to the vacant seat next to me in the corner. He saw me this time and also smiled, he also gestured at me as if saying "hey" and then took a step forward to reach his destination.

There was something wrong with his walking I couldn't figure it out, but he seemed to have a minor difficulty with his gait while walking towards me to grab the seat next to me.

While putting his bag off of the shoulder he looked at me and that was the moment where I realized I was looking at him since the time he entered the class and I'd missed whatever the professor said, I gathered my sentience back and looked straight to the theatre where the professor was continuing.

"This time the chairman and I decided the pattern of delivering lectures based upon…"

"Thank you." he sat down and said,

"I'm Avinash, Avinash Patil. I'm coming from Bangalore and had grown up there only. I was late because I got lost in the building while looking at the architecture and departments, thank you to save this seat, I would've been standing the whole lecture otherwise as the seats in the back are already occupied. What's your name?

Though I heard him formerly through the gate asking for allowance to enter, Yet, for a moment I replayed his voice in my head as it had a unique tone and supple texture when heard from near, it felt like I was talking to a well-built, 6ft altitudinous 5-year-old agitated toddler telling me about himself and curious to make a new friend so asking me questions to start a chat.

"Hey...," I said.

Chapter-4

"...I'm Avantika, Avantika Rao, mention not about the seat. It had been vacant so I used it to put my bag on it but now as you've come, it's yours"

Just this much?" he asked "I mean! Is that all you have to say? Come on! I know you must have a backstage story too before being now, so tell me where you're from?" He asked.

"HEHE! A backstage story huh! Yeah, because we all have one. Well, I am native, my father always wanted me to be an astronaut but yet I am here because I always see myself being a surgeon one day. Rest, I haven't seen any departments or infrastructure yet, because I was little late today, so straightway came into the class but I hope to see it soon after classes, thank you." I replied.

"Oh, Beautiful native of lovely city huh! One must've been really lucky to be sharing this place with a native such as you, HAHA" he mocked at me (for what I assume it to be)

"Of course! People residing here are really lucky and I bet you'll love this place too. I can assure you by being a native of this place, also it's a great place to explore oneself" I said.

"That's great! I liked your assurance as I am going to be a visitant for almost the next 5 years here, and my free bird nature never let me sit silently for this long, I am fervent for adventures and meeting new people around. Would you like to help me to do that?" he asked.

"Surely, however nowadays I'm planning to spend more of my spare time in library to gather facts about our medical college neither I've made any friends to hang out with so far. Also, I am uncertain whether I know much about worthy sightseeing spots or places worth exploring even though I am a native of this place so I think I might not be the right person to ask to join. I feel you're injured too so it might be indeed worse to your pain to go on exploration operation this early, let yourself heal first."

I incontinently realized how I went bonkers once I added about his injuries, he might suppose that I'm an observant and observes things unnecessarily and at this point, it was about him. Once I observed he was floundering with pain in the back while he moved towards the seat and while he settled himself in the chair next to me.

Of course! How am I able to even expect an arbitrary new person to be aware of my trait to be an extra hand for the people in pain and be a creature of habit about suffering with others. Now I'm embarrassed like nothing and just want to dive into the

anatomy book on my desk so deeply that nobody would find me and try to settle a conversation with me for now.
But he continued...

"Back then, during my medical entrance exam days, I was at my home and was studying with my best friend for a few days for exams, I had shooting pain in my back one night, it had been unbearable and I couldn't even move my hand to reach for something to drop down to make noise for attention neither could I struggle to find my phone in that terrible pain to call someone. I just laid there and shrieked for once which only amplified the pain but it had been also heard by my friend sleeping next to me, he then woke up and saw me in pain, then I fainted.
The next time when I opened my eyes I was hospitalized, my father together with others was sitting on the bench next to my bed in the hospital. I called him, "PaPa" he suddenly looked at me and came near to me, he asked, "how are you now?" though I was still scarified by that demon of pain, yet I didn't want to let him realize my suffering, so I said, "□□□ □□□ □□□ □□□□" ("I'm fine, father").

After a while, the doctor came for a visit and told us that I have spinal stenosis, which needs to be operated soon." He said.

Chapter-5

"Oh, I'm deeply sorry, I had no idea you were having such a terrible happening in the past. If I'd know I'd never.... "I said, as I was proceeding with my sympathy (because this is what I've always thought that can comfort one's suffering) that I generated within that moment, the time when I came across about his suffering, but was interposed by him.
"I didn't say that I didn't enjoy that,..." he said amazingly with a grin on his face.

I kept silent along with the confusion over what he just said. How can someone enjoy the pain one suffered? The only thing I could figure out was that he meant he enjoyed his pain. I was eager to hear about what he had to say succeeding and likewise, the moment came.

He continued... "The time when I was going through that diabolical pain, be it pre or post laminectomy operation it sensed like as if my body was on fire or hundreds of electric shocks in one, of course. I was feeling that I won't ever be able to come out of its hands and that I would die of such painful suffering, In the coming moment I even fainted

But as soon as I set up myself alive in the bed of that hospital with my family sitting next to me, I had this consummation of how suffering can let you make a comeback as an indeed stronger person. Suffering is a lesson as well as a medal you won in life. Suffering can teach you going through delicate times alone, it can change you in and out and you'll never be the same.

You'll come out as a person with strength who knows how it feels to suffer from pain. In this way, you're chosen by God to handle the strength one receives after suffering. You'll never fear of suffering in life again, rather you'll no way suffer again once you come out of it. Pain may come in cycles of tears and might stay but you'll never see it the same way once you conquered yourself back from the fear of suffering.

You'll learn to smile through the eyes even when your pain piercing your heart. You'll never feel lonely once you learn to live beyond the realm of pain and the domain of suffering. Suffering is the gist of love and the essence of life, it's a gift of God to everyone in one way or another, just that you need to see it that way. Suffering is a path to growing fragile with strength. Suffering makes you ascertain the summary of life" He finished.

It was this moment of my life that people (like me) would love to write about, the boy I just met a few minutes ago has just answered the questions I've been asking myself throughout my life. I realized just then, the moment I'm living through is the moment I'll never forget, be it about the first day experience of the medical college or about meeting this flamboyant boy sitting next to me or getting the answers of my actuality. That boy made everything special about that day.

"....So, with this, we're done for today, the introduction session with all of you has been a fantastic time for me and I am sure all of you may have enjoyed your first day in the college too, here I wish and I hope you all to be a great doctor of the nation one day and a great student throughout these upcoming 5 years. Thank you." Dr. Awasthi ended his lecture.

For the first time in my life, I ever bunked a lecture mentally, I was onto the voyage of life lessons with the boy I just met a few moments ago.

Professor started to pack up his things in his little briefcase and the screen of the projector turned off. Students started to murmur to each other about the lecture! (I assume)

"Hey! This city is indeed a great place for sightseeing! By the way, being a native of this place, it would be opprobrious for me too to not explore it already, what about I give you company and be your exploration partner?" I replied.

He looked at me as if I said something shocking and then smiled. He gestured "yes!".

In my first lecture of the college, I learnt my first lesson and then the professor left the class.

-MIKHIL HOON-

Uttar Pradesh, India.

Mikhil is a Meerut based eminent scholar of MBBS from NCR institute of medical sciences, Meerut.

SEM:- IMA MSN UP/ STATE E-JOURNAL COORDINATOR:- SNO-INDIA/ EDITOR:- THE WRITER'S ALLIANCE/ VOLUNTEER AND PHILANTHROPIST:- KIND BEINGS/ CAUSE AMBASSADOR:- CHOTI CHOTI KHUSHIYAN

He has been a certified delegate of UPMSNCON-21 and has received a mark of honour for the same. He has been an emcee and coordinator of the event – pride hour: a talk event where he got the opportunity to work with a Mumbai based leading oncologist of SIR H.N RELIANCE FOUNDATION, DR. Prasad Raj Dandekar, and has got his share of appreciation and felicitation for it. He is a part-time worker in many NGO where he mainly focuses on needful for strays and people in poverty. He is a published writer and co-author of multiple books and finds his keen interest in traveling, healthcare, photography, singing and graphic designing.

Email: hoon.mikhil.225@gmail.com

Instagram: @mai_mikhil_hoon/ @quills_on_rescue

"MY JOURNEY TO LOVE"

"You cannot pour from an empty cup" - Anon

All my life I felt like a bystander on a side-line watching my own life slowly get away from me! It has been a bittersweet roller coaster that was full of laughter and tears as I faced challenges and got victory over a few!

Don't get me wrong, I have had a beautiful life and wouldn't change a thing except for maybe one. That's the one I feel is a lesson for all of us out there who are taught to love others but never taught how to love ourselves.

From the beginning, I absolutely adored the mirror! It was a constant companion till I had a younger sibling! I don't know over the years when or how I lost my sense of self, till as a teenager I began to slowly shy away from my very best childhood friend the mirror!

There is a lot that went on that lead me to stop believing in myself and feel alienated from the person standing in the mirror! But then I could write a whole book on experiences that resulted me in disliking myself. Yes, you heard me right - I started hating myself!

Why? Cause I didn't look like other girls, who perhaps were slimmer while I had some extra pounds or the girls who could wear better clothes while I had to hide in boyish clothes always a size too big for me.

If you ask me if I was bullied, then the answer is no. I'm fortunate that I never felt bullied but things my family members would say in a joke sometimes made me pull my shirt to hide the extra pounds. And no, I didn't have the most traumatic experiences but I built that trauma in my head!

The truth is that we always perceive what others say according to our own prejudices and perceptions. So, the harmless jokes at family gatherings or being critically looked at when having an extra biscuit made me cower in the shadows!

I don't remember when exactly I started waiting for other people's validation and acceptance to accept myself and feel a temporary relief! I was fighting a battle with myself to love myself or even accept myself completely the way I was!

As time passed my extroverted personality slowly shrunk to someone who would talk to others only when they talked to me! Holding my head down in large crowds and slowly avoiding places with too many people!

I loathed in self-criticism and self-pity wondering if anyone could ever love me or if I would ever be enough for others or anyone at all. I started doing things to overcompensate the way I looked and drowned my sorrow in food only to end up distorting my self-image even more!

It wasn't until 2015 that I hit my personal rock bottom! The good thing is that when you hit rock bottom the only way to go is up. This rock bottom was the start of something new! Till this day I believed that everything that went wrong in my life was because I didn't deserve better!

Oh, what a fool I was at the realisation! It was like an epiphany. I'm kidding. But it was the day I decided that enough was absolutely enough! And hence began my journey to self-love. And boy oh boy it has been the most fulfilling and freeing experience of my whole entire life!

An evening of November 2015, while filling out a random online questionnaire I realised how little I knew myself! That all my life I had seen myself from other people's glasses and I was utterly bewildered! I really knew nothing about myself and decided to find stuff that could help me know myself better!

It was the best decision I ever made. My life! Getting to know myself was fascinating but also painful that it took me almost 25 years to reach here. But I was also somewhat relieved that I was finally on the right path!

It was no cakewalk! Imagine trying to sort almost 20 years' worth of feelings over a shorter span of time. It was a lot of work but I made it a religious practice! I decided to dedicate at least an hour every day to myself. At first, guilt gnawed at the back of my mind because all I remembered being taught was not to ever be selfish and this felt like exactly that. However, I told myself that this was my hour of medication or my hour of therapy, and I needed it for my well-being.

It took a while to work through the entangled mass of thoughts that were all there. But I was able to do it! With a lot of hard work and consistency, giving up seems less painful at times but trust me that some things are worth the pain always. I wanted to give up too when things got tough, but I told myself "one more day".

As days passed, I started knowing myself, what I liked, what made me happy, what was my comfort zone and what was not. I practiced standing in front of the mirror every morning and telling myself that "I loved the woman I had become" trying not to feel like a total alien while doing it! I did it till the "I love you's" became more genuine and felt like a warm cup of hot chocolate on a snowy winter morning!

I got here! Brave enough to write this story while tears of relief and joy gather at the corners of my eyes! I did it and you can too! I'm proud of myself for coming so far and I'm proud of you too! When you feel all alone, read this and remember you are never alone! It's your time to shine, it's your time to be yourself, it's your time to rule!

From one friend to another - I love you and I believe in you to win any battle you are fighting! You are never alone! You are a warrior - Remember that!

~Millin Sangha Gujral

-MILLIN SANGHA GUJRAL-

Delhi, India.

Millin Sangha Gujral is a professional psychologist and an artist. She has worked in the mental health field for almost 10 years now. Millin envisions a world where everyone has easy access to mental health and a world of understanding and acceptance. She is a small business owner of a brand called "Happy Strokes" which works to spread more awareness on mental health, also she involves herself in various projects and conducts workshops on various mental health, self-growth and self-acceptance topics.

Her vision is to see an easy access to mental health even in small towns. She believes that the world always needs more love, acceptance and kindness.

Instagram: @happystrokes.in

"QISSAS FOR COGITATIONIS"

I Give You Tears of Happiness...

She woke up every day, looked at the mirror, went to school, returned home, ate, played, and cried and cried and cried. After every act of the day, she cried. One night she was again crying herself to sleep when a strange-looking woman appeared to her. She understood that this strange being was a magical witch and can help her if she gave her something in return. She said to the witch sobbing. "I want to stop feeling this way ... but each time a lovely moment passes by I urge to hold it tightly in my palms and never let it go. Unfortunately, not being able to do so makes me feel angry and I cry almost the entire day. I want to be happy." The witch looked at her and manifested a glass box and asked, "Do you want to stop the moments passing by?" The girl nodded her head.

She put the girl in the box with a happy moment and sealed the box. the happy moment repeated itself again and again and the girl felt happy for days...but soon she became tired of it.

One another night the girl asked the witch to stop the happy moment and that she wanted to live a normal life again. The witch replied, "You were not ready to let go, and hence I gave you what you wanted but in return, I took away your future happiness and moments."

Hearing this the girl started crying again but since it was in a 'happy-moment box' her tears became 'Tears of happiness' and the Witch said: "There....that is the best I give you, tears when you are happy."

Nothing lasts and hence when you learn to let go, you prepare yourself to cry for something bigger and better… You prepare yourself for growth ...and that's life.

If you ever feel hard to let go, think about the tears of happiness.... maybe someday you'll also find the glass box and if you do.... please open the box and let her go ......

The Red Blanket.

In a cold shabby world, deep in the woods, there lived a boy. He loved his mother but due to unfortunate circumstances, he lost her and hence was left alone to live in this dark space where he could call no one his own. All he was left with was a red blanket given to him by his mother.

The world was never kind to him and having no one to lean on, every night he felt alone and sad. The thunder and the lightning, the storm and the wind made it difficult for him to sleep. The lack of warmth sent shivers down his spine. One such night, he was sitting all by himself in a corner of the small quarter he lived in, patting his own back, forcing himself to sleep. That is when he saw the red- blanket. That night he swaddled himself in the blanket and as soon as he finished wrapping himself, he saw a magical beam shining on it. Suddenly, all the stick figures on the blanket jumped out of it and started dancing. They held his hand and took him to their own world. Some nights it was a world of witches while on others, it was a land of fairies, and on some other nights, there were giants. Thus, each night was a world unknown for the boy, and just like that, his nights felt better and dreamier.

Days passed by, the boy grew older and the blanket started shredding and ruining. Each tear on the blanket became a dent in the boy's dream and soon the boy could no longer use the blanket. This upset him and he started searching for a similar red blanket but unfortunately, none came close. In anger and frustration, the boy said, “If this red blanket wouldn’t have been here, I would have learned to sleep myself. “

Hearing the boy’s angered complaint the red blanket spoke, “Every blanket can be your red blanket if you let it be.”

Everyone in today’s world is searching for such a red blanket. A blanket that would give them solace. That would help them through the harshest times. That would cover them when they cry, and in the end, comfort them and put them to sleep. But here’s a secret, not every blanket needs to be a red blanket. It can be yellow or blue or pitch black or just an embrace of warmth.

Maybe next time when you find a red blanket, you could just offer it to a boy who is still in search of it. And if you don’t have a blanket, you can just spread your arms for him.

Journey to the land of love.

It was about a year ago that Nina broke up her 7-year relationship with her boyfriend. She tried everything possible to overcome the anxiety and depression. Each day she woke up with a cacophony in her head that she was not good enough. She tried pilates, yoga, swimming, and meditation too but to no avail, all she felt was sad and empty.

She thought that maybe it was all because of this place and that she should move away to move on. She tried applying to various cities and countries for a job. Finally, she got one, but today when she boarded the train, she again felt the void. She broke down as she felt helpless. The feeling that she had been pushing away had slowly but steadily consumed her happiness.

She was looking out of the window and thinking about how to let go of these emotions that are unrequited. She was looking at the passing scenes and sceneries which were picturesque but made her dead within. Suddenly every view started fading from her sight and she fell asleep.

She could not figure out if she was dreaming but she saw a mystical creature sitting in front of her she was trying to categorize this creature as a God, Goddess, Demon, or… alien, but none could fit the creature's characteristics into one. Seeing her confused the creature said, "No need to try to understand me, since I am beyond your understanding, rather just let me take you on a journey." Saying so, the creature took her to land, the land was called 'Wealth'. The people on this land were very wealthy, and when Nina saw herself, she was surprised to find herself one among them. She was happy, she could shop for anything and everything. But in her heart, she still felt empty and sad.

She told the creature to take her somewhere better, this time it took her to the land of 'Fame' and lo! She was renowned but as time passed by, she grew sick of it and she asked for another and another and yet another place. Each time she felt confident that she would find peace in a certain land she could no longer take it. She felt as if she was going to fall apart, she sat down on the ground and started crying bitterly, she screamed and cussed about her inability to forget her past.

The creature saw this and said to her," You got everything you wanted yet you could not move on, and do you reckon why were you not able to move on?" Nina looked up at the creature with eyes full of tears. The creature continued "Maybe, you should forget about materialistic ideals and look at life as something to be cherished."

Hearing the creature, Nina hugged herself tighter, every day since her breakup she had been trying to find solace in material things or rather things that could never make her solely happy. She realised that she needed to nurture herself, accept herself, and lastly love herself to move on.

As soon as she realised this she woke up, it was a surreal dream but it can be said that she grew up a lot while she was dreaming. She smiled at the beaming sun rays and happily patted her back, whispering to herself, "You did a great job by not giving up, let me love you for that."

In this fast-paced world, there are many times when we come across obstacles that tear us apart, break us sometimes even ruin us. All that we rely on during such phases is toxic positivity. Stoicism, sometimes even hate ourselves. But let us understand that we all are humans and there is nothing wrong with feeling for ourselves, giving ourselves some love, and validating our feelings. It is self-acceptance that helps us accept the world.

Maybe next time you face a loss in life, you would remember this story and pat your back saying, "You did a great job by not giving up, let me love you for that."

A letter to my readers,

Hope you enjoyed the stories and keep them in mind the next time something breaks you. I do not say that life is fair but I can always say that life is yours and hence how you feel is how your life would project. Hence my dear darlings, love yourself more, if not more then try loving yourself bit by bit every day.

Life is all about those little things, therefore the next time the wind plays with your hair, smile. The next time sun smiles brighter on you, smile back with all the soulful light that you have as an individual. The next time you see the water waves running towards you, run back towards it. When you see your favourite ice cream in the store, buy it, have it, and fill yourself with love.

The next time you see a classmate waving at you wave back at him or her as if it's the first time you have seen them in years. The next time you get your results, if it's a punch on your face, say that you will definitely punch it back the next time and if your results are sweet as honey pat your back and give yourself some credit.

The next time you have a cup of coffee enjoy it, Next time you cook yourself a meal, eat it like a feast and feel loved. Next time you see a children's park maybe go swing a bit, slide a bit, love a bit.

The next time you feel like singing in the shower let nothing stop you. The next time someone treats you bitterly, stand for yourself, next time you face criticism, do not be harsh on yourself rather make yourself understand and thus support yourself.

This life you are living is an opportunity to love yourself more than what you did in your last life, hence cuddle yourself, love yourself and cherish yourself. Once you master this my dear darlings, nothing can stop you.

Loads of light and love and optimism to help you through your tough times….

-P. SHARON BABY-

Maharashtra, India.

Meet Sharon, her writings are small stories to help one through when they feel that nothing can make things right. Being through certain challenges in life she always wondered, if she would ever be able to make it out of here.

There were nights when she actually felt that it's better to give up than to try so hard, one such night she looked at the night sky and saw the half-moon and that is when she realised that though the moon goes through different phases yet there is not one day when the moon does not try shining.

It keeps shining though it's a full moon day or a half-moon day or a crescent it keeps going on and hence on the new moon day people look forward to seeing it back in the sky. The moon never gives up shining nor does it whine saying that it's only a half or a quarter. She says, "The moon knows that it is enough and so should you."

She started writing stories when she understood the fact that in today's world straight advice might be quite difficult to accept sometimes and hence, we should treat ourselves as a child and try to understand these facets of life through stories. Thus, she started her small journey of writing short stories.

"If you ever come across these and if you feel touched by them, then smile, because that would make me feel happy too! Hope you enjoy these jewels!"

Yours,
Sharon B.

Email: shaniazb1608@gmail.com
LinkedIn: Sharon Baby

"MIND TO LIFE - MENTAL HEALTH, LETTING GO AND COPING"

You may be questioning why you have come here. What has it taken for you to end up in this situation? We might remember what happened in the past, hoping we could get back the time we spent trying to change it.

That is our mind protecting us by creating these out-of-body experiences. The mind's intricate and fascinating mechanism's primary function is to keep us safe. The brain transforms experiences into memories like a vault as we go through life to move away from things that feel bad and toward those that feel pleasant.

The brain works overtime to keep you safe after a traumatic experience. It relies primarily on these outdated blueprints, which leave us feeling unsafe even after the threat has passed. Spacing out, picturing ourselves floating in a vast sea of nothingness alone and full of violent voices, only seeming to sink us deeper and deeper until letting go is the only way we think we can get out. We have no choice but to believe that drowning is our only escape.

The more battered we become, the more we begin to give up on this little bubble we were made to believe loves and protects us. It is now no more than a fragile shelter that cracks after every heartbreak, pain, and disappointment. An empty, soulless shell that only exists because we exist.

Heartbreak is the kind of grief that comes in waves, a violent crime that a stranger doesn't always commit. Too familiar yet unfamiliar, only with permission can someone have the key to cut you that deep. It is not the typical pain—but a swift and silent killer because of its unexpectedness. We never think it could happen to us, but then it does. Like a shard of glass in your gut, although not visible, the edges may even dull over time, but it still cuts deeper than it did the first time. It can feel like death, a bereavement that is so catastrophic, leaving you alone to stitch up the pieces that have been ripped out so brutally.

The disappointment weighs the most, like cement drying on your chest—the type of agonizing pain you would not wish on your worst enemy. You don't have to have been in a relationship to feel heartbroken. Some of the deepest scars can come from the ones closest to us. You become consumed after acknowledging this loss since the heartache has now bled into disappointment. You force yourself to swallow your pain and live with the destruction because you feel you predicted the demise you did not want to accept. You saw them through your eyes and not through theirs. And it is impossible to paint someone all over again once you've seen their true colours. You cannot conceal what they have already exposed.

If you could take just one fragment from this passage, it would be that expectations are the thief of joy. You cannot direct every situation that falls into your life. The moment that your expectations for yourself or anyone else fall short in areas beyond your control, you are bound to be disappointed. By expecting these unrealistic outcomes, we give the world the tool to break our hearts.

As cruel as this sounds, we don't realize how easy it is to confuse love with attachment. Most relationships are like the toys we had as kids. Although they may become damaged and broken, and they may even hurt us, we hold on to them; they can still feel comfortable and familiar, and most importantly, they give us something we think nothing else can provide us with. In return, we never want to let go. Distorted attachment is about dependence and fear. It has more to do with self-love than the love people give you. Raw love is love without false attachment because you carry all the love you need. You are not lacking love for yourself; therefore, you can give it to others without expecting anything in return. The first step is to Prioritize self-love; without it, you will always be desiring love and validation from those around you. Nothing will ever be enough to fill the gap that seems to expand the more you open up to someone and give them what you yourself cannot afford emotionally.

Expecting someone to return just a shred of what you have given them could be one of the greatest forms of self-afflicted torment.

Being brave does not mean ignoring our feelings; it means overcoming what you thought you never would've in a million years. It means leaving whatever it is that is causing you pain. Whether that may be a moment, feeling, or person. We have been constrained to believe that "Time will Heal us," but is this true? Even after all this time, the memories still play fresh in your mind. You are surrounded by all of these people, yet you still feel alone. And when you need those comforting words the most, you hear, "I know exactly how you feel." Like a punch to the gut, the painful words strike, scattering around your mind. It can feel like a hollow void between their world and yours. The distinctness is evident. The feeling can be described as never-ending exhaustion. Each movement feels carefully calculated and communicated with your body that seems to weigh more than triple your size. Still, even then, thinking is emotionally draining, like moving through deep dark treacle with no end in sight. It is an endless ocean in the abyss with no rest. The nightmare cycle continues. You are just existing, not living…

Our darkest thoughts seem to linger. Following us, echoing in the furthest parts of our minds. Forgetting and distracting ourselves seems like the best solution at the time. Like a numbing agent, the bandage can stop the bleeding but for how long? We need to ask ourselves why the brain pushes us towards diversions when experiencing higher levels of anxiety or depression. Regardless of your vice being food, substance abuse, social media, work, or even relationships. The dilemma is that distractions are not always healthy or beneficial. Nobody can binge on food, alcohol, or television forever. In fact, doing so is dangerous. These behaviours eventually become habitual in your brain. You'll eventually need more and more of them to achieve the results you are so desperately craving. Distracting yourself is just a temporary fix that may feel good at the moment, but sooner than later, your dark thoughts catch up with you, and reality does kick in. We must find a way out and a reason to keep going, a coping mechanism that keeps the switch on. But is there a right or wrong way to deal with our emotions? What do we do if this switch no longer exists?

There are countless unanswered questions; hovering around them is the key that could help us escape these intrusive thoughts. You have faced obstacles no one else can envision, battles you have won because you are here today to tell the story. Those moments have shaped you in ways no one has understood, and perhaps they will never understand, so why should you give up now?

We might wish there was a step-by-step manual that could magically wipe away our worries and stresses, a rope that could miraculously pull us from that same vast sea of nothingness. We don't realize this, but if it is so difficult to forget pain, how would we even think to remember sweetness? We have no wound to show for happiness. How would we be able to soak ourselves in the moments of utmost happiness if all we've felt all our lives was happiness? The ups and downs in life make us appreciate the little moments that are so easily overlooked.

The quote "The key lies within us" has been ingrained in our very being ever since we could utter our first words, but we have to admit the harsh reality is that if you don't save yourself first, who will? For most, the hardest thing to accept is that you have to put yourself first. This ideological construct that our culture/society has made us believe "Putting yourself first is selfish" is a myth and an unnecessary insensitive statement. We know we must put the oxygen mask on ourselves first in life-or-death scenarios, so why would this situation be any different? This could be your life-or-death scenario.

Caring about someone. Whether it may be a family member, friend, or partner usually comes with the idea that you give them priority when it comes to your own emotions or decisions. Their desires, needs, and interests become your burden. It makes sense; of course, we want the ones we love to feel heard and understood. We take on their every pain as if it is our own. However, by putting our needs first in whatever way we need to, we can be sure that our care for others will inevitably come from a place of inner abundance and a sense of already having our needs met. As a result, we become more compassionate as partners, relatives, friends, and beyond.

Most of the time, we don't even understand why we feel the way we do. Emotions are highly complex, and sometimes there does not even need to be a reason. However, we can take the necessary first steps by identifying the differences between anxiety and depression, even though the two are deeply intertwined. Anxiety is an elevated rate of emotion on a scale ranging from relaxed and calm on one end to nervous and fearful on the other. Surprising to most, we do require some emotional pain as a motivational force as it can keep us distanced from danger. Depression, on the contrary, is defined as the lack of positive emotion. Around 1989 psychologist Paul Meehl accurately described depression as the relative absence of "Cerebral joy juice," foreshadowing our present neurobiological insight.

On the other hand, Mania is characterized by a surplus of positive emotions. Your positive emotions are anchored in a neurobiological reward system; they steer us towards what is best for us in the same regard that emotional distress guides us away from harm. As a result, both depression and anxiety foster detachment; anxiety can encourage withdrawal while depression removes the motivating force to engage. That can explain why a depressed person can typically confront the dual dilemma of an increased positive sense of well-being while decreasing negative feelings.

Like our physical health, mental health is not constant. Our psychological state is constantly moving on the scale from one end of the spectrum to the other. If you could take anything with you from reading this, it would be, "Allow yourself to feel whatever it is you want to feel in the moment." This can be done by being conscious of all your emotional responses. Take note of what makes you feel disheartened, overwhelmed, or angry in your life. This can make it easier to understand the patterns of behaviour you then display. By understanding these behaviours, we can then predict the outcome of situations we need to stay away from that may have caused us trauma and pain in the past. When we communicate our emotions appropriately, we also inform those around us if they have crossed our boundaries. This can create barriers that protect us from the chaos that surrounds us daily.

We can find ways to regulate our stress by making it the norm to unwind, to cope with the demands of life. Mindfulness, meditation, and workouts are some examples of these. Evidence now indicates that the relationship we have with the environment contributes to its significant influence on our well-being. The phrase "Connectedness" is now commonly used to illustrate the ideal relationship. Nature has been associated with a multitude of benefits, including enhanced attention, reduced stress, overall better mood, and decreased risk of psychological conditions.

It is important to consider that even people with "good" mental well-being can suffer from emotional challenges. External causes of mental illness are very common. This may be due to genetic disorders or temporary chemical imbalances in the brain. Tension and difficulties at school or work can precipitate or worsen the mental condition.

Please consult your doctor if you have ongoing emotional distress. That doesn't seem to be getting better. Remember that seeking help does not mean you have failed. As humans, we are allowed to get the necessary professional help when we feel like we are unable to help ourselves. Attempting to deal with mental illness can feel like you are alienated. The feeling of complete isolation can be extremely difficult. And dealing with the battle that is in your head alone will not make it any easier.

Getting the help, you need means creating a network of support that recognizes your situation. Together, they can provide appropriate and helpful guidance. You are not alone.

You've come this far and might wonder what my final words are for you.

"Allow suffering to cascade through you like a river passing by the mountains; it will impair and form new streams, but the new self will emerge even better than the last" -Reem Haroon.

-REEM HAROON-

England, United Kingdom.

Reem Haroon, the Author of "Mind to Life", is an exceptionally accomplished published Co-Author and highly awarded writer. The acclaimed researcher and psychologist received her B.A. in Psychology with honours from the University of Plymouth in the United Kingdom. Originally from Sudan, Reem has an immensely diverse background; from being an adventurer travelling the world to advocating for mental health, she aims to go to lengths to overcome the stigma associated with mental health and empower those struggling with emotional and mental turmoil.

Email: reemharoon99@gmail.com

LinkedIn: Reem Haroon

Facebook: Reem Haroon

Instagram: @lunamoonx.1

"SCARS OF FOMO"

FOMO

The little girl sat down
Sweating, in her school uniform.
Fumbling for the TV remote;
She found solace in her dorm.

The birds chirped away
At an aesthetic sunset.
She played & laughed & danced;
It was a happy vignette.

Snatching other's lunch at school
Was her favourite pastime.
She wasn't "missing out" on anything;
Contentment was sublime.

Time eventually flew
As phones became "smart".
Reluctantly, she adapted
As she had to do her part.

The digital revolution had repercussions,
Lethargy & laziness dominated the scene.
Languid demeanour meant that
"Face-to-face" became less keen.

An "Iron Curtain" was formed
As 2 realities became prominent.
The "actual" reality diminished,
While the virtual turned predominant.

In-person activity inhibited
While 'gram caused a storm.
"Did you try uploading stories?"
"Reels" became the norm.

Quietly she snapped a page
From her favourite novel.
The picture was crisp
As she ate her Belgian waffle.

"Agatha Christie, you beauty!"
She clicked "Upload & Post!"
"2 million likes", she saw a reel;
15 likes was all her snap could boast.

Her friends uploaded stories & reels
Of mountains, stadiums and lakes.
"It's cool!", some crossed the line
What they posted were just fakes.

She saw a myriad pictures of
Her friends, partying at clubs.
Being the conservative type,
She read & stayed home instead.

Tokyo, Paris, London and LA;
English, Dutch and The Swiss;
Gradually, a thought crept in;
"Am I missing out on this?"

"Did you try this?"
"What! No? Really?"
"What are you even doing?"
"Go, get a life!!"

Words kept reverberating in her ears;
Frustrated, she caused daily fuss.
Virtual reality was now "real"
As FOMO became ubiquitous.

Relinquishing her misery,
She went with her confidant.
The atmosphere was electric
But she wasn't nonchalant.

Watching every step of hers
As people came by.
Intoxicated, disgusting and weak;
She regretted of giving it a try.

It just wasn't her at all,
All pompous and vociferous.
Sedate, calm and reserved
Was what she really was.

The realization eventually struck in
As she was all losing it.
Gallantly, she asked herself,
"Was this all worth it?"

She had forgotten herself,
'Cause that's what FOMO does.
"Was it worth it?" - NO!!
'Cause it was just a buzz!

-ROHAN CHHABRA-

Allahabad, India.

This here is Rohan, he is a passionate software engineer. Currently, he's pursuing his Master's in "Computer Science". Though he is a techie by profession, his heart has a special place for words and poetry as a hobby. Occasionally, he writes poems mostly on emotional topics as he believes that they are the best way to make an impact in society. With this poem, he aims to emphasize the need to prioritize mental wellness, especially during this pandemic when we as a society need each other more than ever, he states.

The generation in which he grew up was when social media got nurtured from a small child to the beast it is today. He has seen the boon and bane of it and he believes a lot of FOMO (Fear of Missing Out) can be attributed to the way we consume social media today. FOMO is something our generation experiences everyday and, in his opinion, it is never ever healthy as it causes so much mental grief. In this fast-paced world today when professionalism is ubiquitous, one should try to know themselves throughout and appreciate themselves. Wanting what others are having seems attractive but it is never going to be satisfactory if it doesn't align with who you really are, he adds. He hopes with this small poem, he is able to disseminate this message.

Email: rohan23chhabra@gmail.com

LinkedIn: Rohan Chhabra

Instagram: @rohan23chhabra

"DISABILITY TO ABILITY – OVERCOME MENTAL HEALTH"

Studies and researches have time and again indicated that people with disabilities are at higher risk of mental health issues compared to their non-disabled counterparts. In general, people with a disability report poorer general health and higher levels of psychological distress than people without a disability.

Learn how to deal with stress. Try to make your life more purposeful. Every moment is precious for each and every one of us. I had personally experienced stress due to my visual challenges in life. To overcome I tried to occupy myself with other activities. The best thing I chose is music and technology.

Music is a powerful tool. It can help boost your mood as well as cure a broken heart. For centuries, music has played an important role when it comes to our ability to cope with life's greatest highs and lows.

At a very young age, I started my Music journey. This improved my confidence, diverted my mood, my mind and made me stronger. I'd recommend to anyone that if things aren't going right, and you don't know what to do, just turn up some good music, and jam out for a few minutes before attempting to figure everything out again.

My journey with music was going on well but I had struggled in my education, writing with slate and stylus was so boring, braille education was a must for me which was not interesting to travel. At this time technology came into my life. I started learning how to operate the PC and learned my lessons on a computer which was more interesting for me and that's how I completed my studies well.

Music was travelling with me throughout and technology too. This made me step onto the next level. I started using both and started developing music through technology. I self-trained music production tools and customized them for my use. Digital music technology, electronic effects, sound engineering, recording and broadcast of music, design and construction of musical instruments, editing and mixing the tools available to create contemporary music on your computer. Music became my passion and Technology my third eye. This made me live a life with independence and dignity. I would recommend that technology is more important, especially for a person with visual impairment. Screen reading software's and talking software's help them explore the system and educate themselves in many ways and travel with ease in their day-to-day activities. I also educate people with visual impairment on how to explore technology, use computers, cell phones and other electronic devices independently.

Today I would proudly say that I'm an independent artist running my own music studio with the latest technology. Released music albums and into music production and played the role of a music director for many projects. My journey as a Music Director started on a trending YouTube channel. Through this, many came to know my music. My first album in the movie industry was released as a Music Director after 7 years of hard work and challenges. I was known to many through this album, was overloaded with calls and messages, the news channels approached me, my interviews came in many channels and celebrities started visiting my home studio. I became viral on all social media platforms.

My family means a lot to me, my mom and dad are always my strong pillars of support. They taught me how to be independent, how to move on, how to overcome, how to face the world and there I am today.

Life requires a considerable amount of physical and mental effort. Some are fortunate enough to have everything prepared for them but for some people, life is a hardship however I chose not to let life get me down. I chose how to be positive and confident to overcome my obstacles. My struggle symbolizes a compass, it correctly shows the path of my life and it serves as a force of motivation that pushes me to prevail over my struggles. When you have a struggle, you will learn to solve a problem. If one solution doesn't work, it's okay. Go back to the drawing board and try another.

Find the person in you despite all of the challenges; bring it out to the world. Nothing is impossible, all need is self-confidence. To accomplish the most difficult tasks, we need to put in a lot of hard work and it's very important not to think about our weaknesses, just overcome that challenge and keep moving forward.

In this world, there's no such thing as CHANCE! With our own ideas, will and ability, we can create a number of chances, circumstances and the desired atmosphere to achieve the toughest goal in our life.
Take "DIS" out of "DISABILITY" and make it ABILITY.

"I have no eye vision but, I have no limits to my vision"
–Rudolph Godson.

RUDOLPH GODSON-

Tamil Nadu, India.

This is Godson, born with Retinal degeneration, lost vision at a very young age but moving on with a desire to achieve many things in life. He's an independent artist. By God's grace, he has overcome the challenge and has excelled in becoming a great Musician and Programmer today. At a very young age, he learnt to play 5 musical instruments, the piano, recorder, drums, "*tabla*" and guitar. His favourite instrument is the piano. He started composing many tunes of his own and released his 1st album at school when he was 17 years. He learnt braille education at school and computers to pursue his studies.

In college, he won the Best Musician Award for 3 consecutive years (Hat trick). He started a music band named "CheckMate". He is the first visually challenged student of "Madras Christian College, Chennai" to get elected as Cultural Convenor. He strongly believes that the almighty has given him all these talents. He would always love to play in his Church during Sunday Services.

He started posting music videos on social media…YouTube, Facebook, etc.. and took up the challenge of posting popular songs every day for 100 days non-stop. This challenge was to prove nothing is impossible. This reached out to some of the public and he came up in news articles like "Decaan Chronicle", "Vikatan" and other local production companies. Godson released a music album as a music director which was Top Trending No.1 on YouTube and Twitter.

Instagram: @godsonrudolph
Music: Criminal Crush - Official Song | Ashwin Kumar | Anirudh Ravichander | Tanya | Godson | Ruthra |Anand
Youtube: Godson Rudolph

"YOU"

Door

You stand in front of it.
You hate it.
You want to leave
but you say a prayer
and knock.
There's no answer.
Your heart's in your mouth
for what's behind it.
Is he lying naked
in a pool of his own vomit
room reeking bitter
or is she lying
barely all there
failed pills scattered.
What do you really want?
kick it open
or not care for once
and run.
You stand in front of it.
Something
slams shut
inside you.

Knife

You hold it
over the cake.
Stuck between
their row and screams.
Can you see
through your tears?

She grips it.
He in front of her.
Your feet go numb
and you're alone.
Will you move
before the blow?

You clutch it.
Staring too long
at the cold steel
against your flesh.
Will it somehow
numb the pain?

Trash

They call you
it.
Again
and again.
You believe
it.
You change.
Their words change.
You're no longer
it.
But why
do you still stink?
Because now
nobody calls you
it.
So you do.
You
call yourself
it.
They made sure
you still believe
it.
Voices inside.
You still
stink.

You

Cold soul.
Colour yourself
the warmest shades
of hope.
You are purple.

Silenced soul.
Listen
to the notes of beauty
within you.
You are music.

Choked soul.
Let your words
pour out
in sheets of love.
You are a book.

Gutted soul.
Open your eyes.
Your story unfolds
in polaroids of strength.
You are a movie.

Not door, knife or trash.
It
is you
who decides.

Most of us
are constantly on that journey towards
understanding, finding, accepting and loving ourselves.
It'll take time. And patience. But please hang in there.
Sure, the climb won't be easy.
It'll be hard. And sometimes sad and lonely.
But find it in yourself to hold on.
Remember that when you finally make it to the summit,
the view will be worth
everything you went through.

-SANDRA V JOSE-

Kerala, India.

Sandra, a perplexed person who's still trying to understand herself. She loves to write because she can express herself better that way. Music, books and movies are the three things she's most passionate about. They make her world beautiful she states. And of course, there are a handful of people in her life that she honestly can't imagine having never met. They were at the right place at the right time, and that made all the difference because it made her the person she is today.

Email: **sandravjose@gmail.com**
LinkedIn: Sandra V Jose

"YES, I AM DIFFERENT, AND THAT'S THE WAY I AM!"

To the world who stigmatised me,

I am Eve, 21 years old. I have Down's syndrome. By now, you all very well have imagined the way I look. Yes, I have a flattened face, almond eyes, small ears, short neck, and small hands and feet. But do you know why I am different from you all? I have an extra chromosome than most of you. Typically, a baby is born with 46 chromosomes, but I was born with an extra one, and this additional copy of the chromosome changes how I look, and my brain develops. It causes a lot of physical and mental health issues for me.

My struggle started the day my mum came to know I was going to be born with Down's syndrome. Though everyone around her suggested she get me aborted, she took a stand. Her pregnancy was not easy; mentally, she didn't get much emotional support from her closest kin, but my dad stood by her like a rock.

Finally, I arrived. I was named Eve for its meaning, the source of life. That's what I am for my parents.

My birth was half the battle won. When my mother held me for the first time, she experienced overwhelming love and joy and the fright of not knowing whether she would be able to handle a child with special needs. Most importantly, will society accept me the way I was?

From birth till now, I have been judged based on my diagnosis, not my abilities and uniqueness. My parents are being questioned and mocked for their decision to bring me into this world. But, they never gave up on me.

Yes, kids like me are slow learners. I reached my milestones later than other kids, but that does not make me an outcast. What If I uttered my first word when I was two, or I didn't start to sit till I was one.... What's the rush? Every Individual has her own pace to develop and learn.

Unlike you all, it takes me time to express and read. I am not that quick to use spoken language, but despite patiently listening to me, you mocked me, shattering my confidence.

Your giggles and laughter on my stutter, your jokes on my looks, your silent gaze...makes me feel depressed. Throwing my books, hiding my things, and bullying me was fun for you, not me.

I remember your hoots when I got my first period. Unaware and bewildered, I spent hours in the washroom, sobbing. Nobody came to my rescue.

Now at the age when you all are in universities, I am still in high school, struggling with my basics.

The road to my success is way too long. The biggest roadblock in it is the attitude of society towards me. All I need for you all is acceptance. Yes, I am different, but that's not my fault. It is the way I was born. I wish I could have the choice to be born as Normal as most of you.

In the end, I will just say.....

Next time you meet someone like me, think beyond our imperfections.
Look at the smile that goes till eyes.
Look at our eyes that long for a friendly gaze,
A gaze that has no pity, but acceptance!
Let us be your friend, companion.

We will not disappoint…
We love to giggle and laugh.
Nobody is born perfect, and neither am I, not you.
But together, we can make this world a better place for all.
Where the mind is beyond the shackles of discrimination.
Where the world is open for us all.
Where everyone can walk with their head held high.
Give me space in your hearts.
And you will see I am also a human being
Yes, I am different, and that’s the way I am.

-SANJANA KAPOOR-

London, United Kingdom.

Sanjana Kapoor is a content writer by profession. She has been working in the field for more than eight years. Writing is not only her profession but her passion too. It all started when her best friend moved out of the city, and she penned down the first letter to her; pouring out her heart to her.

From letters to friends, to letters to editors, article writing, blogging... she just loves every bit of it. She holds a Master's degree in journalism, from BBK DAV College, Amritsar. Currently, she lives in London with her husband and six-year-old son.

Instagram: @sanjana_k1432

"THE OCEAN OF LIFE"

Introduction

For years I hid my mental health issues. I learned to wear a mask and hide my pain. I thought it would go away, but it never did. Instead, it fed on my fears, hang-ups, and insecurities. Years went by, and I realized that I could not afford to bury the hurt anymore. I didn't know where to start, and I wasn't ready to tell anyone about my pain. The thought of death began to stick in my mind like chewing gum. For a moment in time, I thought that death was my only way to escape the pain; I was wrong!

I needed to go back to the beginning and start examining my life. I began to see that my parent's needs superseded my own. They failed to teach me proper coping skills and other valuable life lessons, but they showed me how to pour the perfect cocktail and put my seven-year-old self to bed while experiencing our city's underbelly. I saw my childhood for what it was and how it affected my inner child. I learned to parent my inner child and learned valuable coping skills, but I knew I needed to break the cycle. Slowly I started to heal and found my passion; writing. It was freeing to let my feelings bleed from my pen; I didn't have to hold onto the pain anymore. I found people who taught me how to craft my words into a work of art. My poem, *The Ocean of Life*, shows where my mind was, the struggle I was dealing with, and how I learned to "let go" of the pain and live with it and start a new life with a new mindset.

The Ocean of Life.

I failed to get help with my trauma.
I thought a trip to the therapist's office would make me weak and vulnerable.
Now I am in the middle of life's storm, swimming for survival.

Stuck in the vast ocean of life, the shore is miles away, but I'm ready for a new life.
I didn't know where to start, so I put my head in the ocean water and started the swim.
Swimming against the current is tiresome, I just started, and I want to give up.
The salt water stings my eyes, and I start to cry.
I'm surrounded by water, but my throat is so dry.
Am I dying of thirst? I'm not going to give up, so I swim harder.
Minutes or hours, I pick up my head; it seems like I'm going nowhere in this vast ocean.
How did I get here? Why did I let my trauma define me?
Is my fate the same as Icarus? Did I fly too high and become reckless?
No! Icarus had a father who gave him life lessons.
Father taught me how to pour the perfect cocktail.
I scream out for help; I'm ready to change my life.
There are no lifeboats to hear my pleas.
I feel the aquatic life nipping at my toes, waiting for their next meal.
I hate that this is how my life turned out.
I use all my hate and start to swim. Will it get me closer to shore?
I'm exhausted, and the hate has been purged, but I'm no closer to shore.
Now what? Love? Love doesn't last; I need a miracle.
I've become Winslow Homer; I'm lost at sea.
I'm a dead man, waiting for the perfect wave to pull me under.
My body cramps; I know the end is near, so I swim as hard as possible.
I swim until I can't. There is no more swimming; now, I'm treading water to survive.
I'm bobbing up and down like a cork. My eyes stare at the clouds.
Then I go underwater; I kick my legs harder for a breath of air.
Why am I fighting destiny? I open my mouth, and a rush of saltwater fills my mouth.

The salty water runs down my oesophagus, and my lungs fill with water.
This is it, one more glug, and I'm fish food.
A knock against the back of my head brings me to my senses.
A decomposed piece of driftwood gives me an option.
Learn to live with the pains in life or die.
I held onto it as my grandma held me as a newborn.
I refuse to make another mistake in life and accept the gift.
I start to kick towards hope that I cannot see but know it is there.
I make vows and promises that everything will be different if I get to shore.
It wasn't easy, and the swim to shore felt like years, but I made it.
I let go of all the pain and trauma and left it in the ocean.
I refused to let go of the piece of driftwood; it is a part of who I am now.
I whittled the wood into a walking stick, and together we are walking in a new life.

-STEVEN DEE KISH-

Nevada, United States of America.

5625 Corbett St, Las Vegas, NV 89130 · 702-232-8564 · kishsd@nv.ccsd.net

Steven Dee Kish is a writer who lives in Las Vegas, Nevada. He has endured childhood trauma and is a survivor of suicide. His writing shows what life is like, when someone is living on the edge of madness/sorrow. When Steve shared his writing with the public, it was received with positivity and people confirmed that they too hurt, but were unwilling to "put themselves out there", but people found comfort that he was hurting, just like them. Steven's YouTube channel *Address the Elephant in the Room* has published poems from him. Currently, twenty-five poems have been published since 2021. Steven's poems have been printed in *Pure Slush Books (Lifespan Vol 3, 4, & 5 AU). Night Picnic (Volume 4 issue 3). Wingless Dreamer Anthology (Dawn of the day, Book in black, Snowflakes & mistletoes, and My Cityline). Voices from the fire (Vol 8);* and many other great publication houses.

Instagram: @address_the_elephant_intheroom

YouTube: Address the Elephant in the Room

"PHYSICAL HEALTH IMPACTING MENTAL HEALTH"

It has been known for a significant period of time that there is a link between mental and physical health both influencing each other to a significant degree many people with compromised mental health for example having clinical depression experiencing physical fatigue or actual body ache but as mentioned this effect goes both ways and it is possible to better your mental health by resolving your physical health.

Sleep hygiene

One physical aspect that can impact your health is sleep. A lack of quality sleep can cause a person to become easily agitated and generally lower your mood and affect your memory this change in personality also can cause damage to relationships as these people may come across as impatient and unfriendly which can further serve to damage their mental health possibly becoming isolated from social circles. It can also lead to weight gain which can cause further damage through a drop in confidence. It can also cause a crippling reduction in energy not too long ago I suffered from insomnia for months on end and on one occasion I fell straight to the floor the exhaustion caused by sleep deprivation led me to lie there face down for over an hour trying to summon any energy or motivation to get up whereas in the past I would usually. Thankfully this can be helped to have a consistent sleep routine while also abstaining from stimulants and light before sleep can be a great help you should make sure to wind down for an hour before bed or you may find yourself staring at the ceiling unable to get any meaningful rest.

Diet

Another major factor that impacts mental health which is unfortunately rarely mentioned is diet a nutrient deficient diet can cause many ill effects one unfortunate victim of this was a close family member of mine who became deficient in vitamin B12 rendering him almost unable to form any coherent sentences for someone who prided themselves on their wit it was quite degrading and had noticeable impacts on his confidence however this was easily fixed with a supplement. The difference these seemingly minor factors make is staggering. Another nutrient which influences mental health is omega 3 which is found in foods like ground up flax and chia seeds with low omega 3 being associated with a higher likelihood of depression.

With nutrition I believe it is important not to be too strict or diligent as that can lead to disorders like orthorexia it is best not to overcomplicate just make sure you eat a variety of foods and try to stick to whole foods however, I would recommend a b12 supplement as it is difficult to get consistently from whole foods and make sure it's a realistic diet you can stick to.

Exercise

Exercise reduces anxiety and depression and can improve self-esteem. Many people know this but often fail to implement it. The best way to implement this is to start small like a 5-minute walk once a day many people make the mistake of trying to follow a fitness models routine and then waking up the next day and not being able to get out of the bed the next day then come to the conclusion, they are allergic to exercise and give up. It is also ideal to find a form of exercise you enjoy for some it could be dancing, boxing or even going on a walk through the woods and appreciating nature for me I found resistance training and martial arts to be ideal as it made me feel empowered as I could move in ways that seemed almost impossible at first glance and the process of progression becoming able to move objects that were once unmovable for me helped to keep me motivated and consistent.

How this helped me

This is a part of mental health which many unfortunately overlook but for me, it made all the difference when I tried to improve my mental well-being, I struggled to even think how to help myself it seemed like an impossible obstacle that I had no hope of overcoming but by improving my physical health and creating good habits I obtained the ability to change my situation and actually make a difference to my quality of life. The ability to improve my mental health by improving my physical health for me gave me the power to influence my mental health and overcome one of the most difficult trials I have ever faced and I hope the information here will allow you to do the same.

-ANONYMOUS-

Verses Kindler Publication

Reach us through our website -

https://www.verseskindlerpublication.com/

For more information visit our Instagram or Facebook page.

9 789356 050471

Printed at Repro India Ltd.